THE BAKERY BOOKING

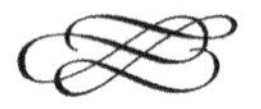

MORGAN UTLEY

Published 2021 by Next Chapter

Edited by Tyler Colins

Cover art by CoverMint

To the sisters in my life. To my sisters, Kirstin and Halee, who are the best sisters and the best friends a girl could ask for. To Mom and Aunt Kylee, who were the greatest examples as sisters and who I constantly look up to. To my sister in-laws, Mary and Brooklyn, who accepted me as their new sister with open arms and I'm so grateful for them.

CHAPTER 1

It was a cloudy, gray morning when I woke up in my old room to the sound of a very loud alarm clock going off. After a couple minutes of lying in bed, debating whether or not I should get up, I rose from the bed to get ready for school. Luckily, I remembered to pack an extra pair of underwear. Last weekend, when I stayed at my mom's house, I forgot a pair and had to dig around in some old drawers.

I found an old pair of small, pink polka-dotted underwear to wear. I'm pretty sure they were from middle school. I was unable to go to my apartment before class to change, so I had to wear them all day long. Due to the size I was uncomfortable and had to make frequent visits to the bathroom to try and adjust to make them more comfortable. I promised myself I would never forget underwear again and to throw out my old delicates next time I was at my mom's.

I pulled some clothes out of my backpack to change. I threw my wild, wavy blonde hair up into a high ponytail, trudged down the stairs and decided to do some last-minute studying before class. I opened my laptop, pulled out my books and notes, and started working on an essay for my business class.

"Rosie, are you coming into the bakery today? I have a big

cupcake order I need to finish, and I'm going to need help closing up," my mom asked as she put her purse over her shoulder and picked up her keys.

I had been so engrossed in my writing, I hadn't heard my mother walking down the stairs and practically jumped out of my seat. "Geez Mom, a little warning next time!" I gasped and put my hand over my heart to try and stop it from beating so fast.

"Sorry, honey, I didn't think I was going to scare you,!" she chuckled and opened a kitchen cupboard to pull out a protein bar.

"Sure," I answered sarcastically and then changed my tone so she knew I wasn't teasing. "I just have a couple classes this morning, and some studying to do, and then I'll head over afterwards. You know what, I'll just eat my lunch and study home, and then head over to the bakery afterwards," I decided and stood up from the barstool in front of the kitchen counter and gathered my things.

"Thanks, sweetie. I think your sister is coming in too. She said she had a test this morning and then she was meeting Jake for lunch. Those two, I tell ya. I think I hear wedding bells," my mom sang.

She was a pretty woman, with curly blonde hair and hazel eyes that quite frequently had dark circles around them from getting up early to open the bakery. Despite her always looking tired, she had more energy than I had in my pinky. Growing up, I felt like I struggled keeping up with her, rather than the other way around.

"Oh boy." I rolled my eyes and followed her out the back door to climb into our cars.

"I can finally make my dream wedding cake for her! A stark white cake with pink gum paste roses cascading down the side. Oh, and it's going to be a chocolate cake with strawberry frosting and fresh strawberries in the center!" she rambled off as we both opened our car doors and put our bags into the passenger seats.

"Are you sure that's what Lily wants? I thought she always wanted funfetti cake with fondant swag draping all down the front of the cake?" I asked and smiled at her, wondering if she caught my hint of teasing.

"She does not!" she piped and made a face at me.

I shrugged my shoulders, "You never know! That girl changes her mind all the time."

"It's true!" she called, "I have to get to work. Tell Lily to call me, I want to hear how her date with Jake went. I haven't heard from her all weekend!"

"Okay, I will. Love you!" I called back and climbed into my car and drove to school.

My last comment was true. Lily had changed her major probably three different times within the last couple of years and, for the moment, had decided on becoming a teacher, so she had been taking a lot of education classes. But because she had changed her major so many times, she had a bunch of pointless classes that weren't going toward her degree. She had painting classes when she wanted to become an artist, accounting classes when she thought about becoming a CPA, and even chemistry classes when she thought about being pre-med. Which, I gotta say didn't last long, because she didn't do so hot in chemistry.

For now, Lily was stuck on becoming an elementary teacher. She really liked the idea of playing with kids all day and having a long summer vacation. Unlike my sister, I always knew what *I* wanted to do: I wanted to become a baker and major in business to help my mom run her small business.

For years, I'd watched my mom get up early, head into the bakery and make dozens of cupcakes and cookies, and decorate the most beautiful cakes. She always said that it was her creative outlet, that she could eat and never get bored of it. Every customer was unique and always wanted something different, nothing was ever the same. It was her passion and she loved it, and I grew to love it too.

Once I entered high school, I started getting up early with my mom and helped prepare things for opening. Then I would go to school and right after school go back to the bakery. My mom was constantly working at the bakery and trying to earn her bachelor's degree. She was the hardest working woman I have ever met. During my junior year, she graduated and was able to find a full-time job that she could do from home. Her work schedule enabled her to continue running her bakery and hire more help, which included me.

After I graduated high school, I was able to earn a scholarship that paid for my schooling, and I moved out of the house and started attending Truman University close to home. My sister and I had watched my poor mom struggle financially for years after my dad left. I decided I wanted to leave the house as soon as I could to ease some of her burden, so she could get caught up on bills and life.

The moment my sister graduated high school, she decided to move in with me, so we could split the rent. This left my mom all alone in an all too quiet house, which sometimes left her depressed. My sister and I decided to go visit every once and a while, and spend time with our mom.

This weekend, Lily didn't come to Mom's with me, because she and her long-term boyfriend Jake had a special date planned all day Saturday, and then she had a lot of studying to catch up on. Jake was always hanging out in our apartment, which didn't help Lily's study habits. When she failed a couple of classes her first semester, she made a vow to herself to not stay up late, and make time for studying. This semester, she was doing a little better, but she usually ended up playing catch up on the weekends or whenever Jake was busy doing something without Lily. This happened on rare occasions, but when it did, Lily would get a lot accomplished.

My mom and I had debated whether or not Jake was going to

pop the question this weekend and waited to hear from her, but she never called us. I was tempted to call her and see what was going on, but thought better of it. She and Jake were probably enjoying time together without me in the room.

Lily had been dating Jake since her sophomore year of high school. They met each other on the swim team and immediately hit it off, and had been together ever since. It hadn't, however, always been rainbows and butterflies with their relationship. There had been many growing pains from going through high school and the drama that came with it, deciding which college to attend, whether or not they would remain together, and the plain old relationship drama that came around every once in a while. Nevertheless, through their roller coaster of a relationship, they were still together and loved each other more for it.

I thought Lily and Jake were the cutest couple on the planet. I was secretly hoping that Jake had popped the question to Lily on their special date, but she would have called if that had happened. She loved him so much, she hardly knew what to do with herself. She was constantly talking about the boy and I often wondered if they were ever going to tie the knot. Granted, Lily was only twenty and some would say that they were too young, but in my opinion "when you know, you know".

I never had the opportunity to feel that kind of love. I didn't date a whole lot in high school, and my life became enveloped in the bakery and helping my mom. My dad left us when I was eight and Lily was only six. Mom doesn't tell us a lot about why he left, just that he didn't want to be a dad anymore and wanted to live a life free of responsibility. What I did know was that it broke my mom's heart. She was a stay-at-home mom and hadn't worked since I was born. The moment he left, she knew that she would have to work hard to be able to take care of us.

She found a full-time job working at a grocery store in the bakery department, and after a few years of practicing how to frost cakes and developing her own recipes, she opened up her own side business to make a little extra cash. This all happened while going to night school to earn her bachelor's degree, not to mention, trying to raise two daughters all by herself. That's why I committed myself to working so much in the bakery.

I promised myself to make sure I received an education, so that no matter what, I had something to fall back on, instead of trying to fit it in later in life. I wanted to be prepared for life and its unexpected surprises as best as I could. I chose a relationship with work and school rather than actual human people. Which was a sacrifice I was willing to make for the time being. Once I finished school and figured out a job, *then* I would reevaluate life and go from there. So, I guess in a way, I never gave myself the opportunity to fall in love because I put other priorities first.

Lily didn't have the same view as me, which became frustrating at times. She was all about the boys, the popularity status and being involved in extracurricular activities like sports, choir and attending every high school sporting event. Once Jake entered her life, this only got worse. Her life became all about Jake. Granted, she still worked at the bakery a few times a week, but I could tell she had her attention on something else. She lightened up a little bit after high school, and realized that family and relationships were more important than whether she had gone to the football game over the weekend. But, still, her life revolved around fun and boys, and mine was focused on preparing for a future. Neither were necessarily wrong or right, just different...even if I thought mine was right.

CHAPTER 2

My first two classes were absolutely boring. I sat through a chemistry class that had a lab to follow and it seemed to go on forever. Luckily, I had a partner looking to get into medical school and always did well in the labs. Me, not so much. I felt like I never contributed anything to the work, but my partner was so focused on earning good grades for his applications, he didn't seem to mind me standing there looking like an idiot. The next class was calculus and I ended up taking a surprise quiz, and was grateful that I'd decided to study over the weekend. Otherwise, I might have bombed it. After my classes, I went back to my apartment to study for a test that was coming up in one of my business classes.

I walked into the apartment, and immediately found my sister on the couch with a bunch of tissues and a party-size bag of M&M's sitting on her lap, while watching *Sleepless in Seattle* on the TV.

"Uh, sis? Are you okay?" I walked over and dropped my bags on the ground and looked at her.

Her face was all red and blotchy. Her blonde curly hair was in a messy bun that had hair sticking out every which way, and she was wearing baggy sweatpants. She looked at me and tears started welling in her eyes. I wrapped my arms around her, trying my best to comfort her.

She leaned into me and started crying on my shoulder. I grabbed the box of tissues and put them on my lap so they were easily accessible to her, rather than use my shirt.

Lily grabbed a tissue, and continued to blubber and blow her nose for the next five minutes. Finally, she sobbed, "Jake and I broke up."

"What?" I shrieked and I felt Lily nod her head.

"Yep. During our special date on Saturday. We got into a stupid fight about his parents and one thing led to another. I said, 'Well, maybe you shouldn't be with me, if I make you so unhappy,' and he said, 'Maybe I shouldn't.' Then he brought me home and I haven't heard from him since," she wailed and started crying even harder than before.

"It sounds like you two got just got worked up and you both said things you didn't mean. I'm sure you'll work it out," I said encouragingly.

Lily shook her head. "Usually when we fight, he comes over by now and we make up. But I've tried calling him and texting him and I've gotten no response! It's *really* over this time! I blew it!"

"I'm sure that's not the case…maybe he's busy or just needs time to let off steam. Give it a little bit and it will be okay. I'm sure he will call eventually," I insisted. "You two have been together way too long to give up now."

"You think so?" She looked up at me with red puffy eyes, still full of tears. "You really think he will call?"

"Yes. I think it's all going to be just fine," I maintained and hugged her tighter. "Why don't you go shower, and I'll clean up this mess?"

"Okay, that's probably a good idea. I haven't showered since Saturday morning," Lily admitted and trudged off to the bathroom.

"Yeah, I can tell," I teased and smiled.

She turned and shot me a look. Too bad she wasn't very intimidating too me.

I could tell she was starting to feel a little better already. While she was busy wasting all our hot water, I cleaned up all her nasty tissues, put the candy away and wiped down the coffee table with disinfectant wipes. Once I was done cleaning, I made my sister a smoothie, because I figured she hadn't eaten a healthy thing all weekend, and poured myself some of the extra. I cleaned up the mess, along with the rest of the kitchen and all of Lily's tissues. Feeling a little more relaxed now that the apartment was picked up, I sat on the couch and was able to start studying for my upcoming test.

My sister didn't surface from the shower for about an hour. When she found her way into the kitchen, I stood and followed her. I handed her the smoothie and she smiled, "Thanks, sis."

"That's what sisters are for." I returned a smile and found my way back to the couch and continued studying.

Lily came and sat next to me, and turned her movie back on. "You know, I never thought we would ever actually break up. We've had so many fights over the last few years, so many arguments, I never thought we would ever reach that point and end the relationship. It just blows my mind. I really thought he was the one, Rose."

"You know what? I still think he is. Just give it time," I smiled and held her hand and she continued to watch her movie while I attempted to study.

Boy was I wrong.

A week passed, and she heard nothing. She stayed by her phone, constantly checking it, resisting the urge to call or text him first, but had no luck. She ended up missing a couple days of class, because she was too upset to go. By the weekend, she had made the couch into her bed, and refused to get up. Our mom ended up coming over and staying with us instead, because she knew Lily wouldn't have the heart to leave the apartment.

The next week she went to class, mostly because she had to take a test, but was a complete zombie. She hadn't washed her hair in days; her blonde curls were sticking up all over her head. She had dark purple bags under her eyes from not sleeping, and her face was pale and gaunt from not eating very much. To add to her sad look, she wore baggy sweatpants with paint on them and old high school shirts that had holes in them. It was hard to watch her be so depressed, but she didn't want us to talk to her about Jake. I felt bad too, because I was so sure that Jake would call, and had told Lily not to worry.

On the bright side, she came around the bakery more often and helped Mom and I out, and always closed with us. She insisted that she was wanting to help, but deep down, I knew it was because she didn't want to be at home alone. I couldn't blame her either. She'd been with Jake a long time, and I think she hoped he was going to propose soon.

It had been three weeks since the breakup and we were all sitting on our mom's couch, watching another romance movie. This time, it was *You've got Mail.* One of my personal favorites.

"Guys can be such jerks. It's always their game, always out to make the woman look like a fool. I can't stand it!" Lily proclaimed and threw popcorn at the TV.

"Alright!" Mom picked up the remote and turned off the television. "You have got to get out of this funk!" she declared. "I'm sorry you and Jake had a falling out and I'm sorry you had your heart broken, truly I am. But my darling, you either need to start moving on or go and fix it with Jake. It's been three weeks. Am I wrong, Rosie?" She turned to look at me, expecting me to join in, but I shook my head and raised my arms.

"No way, leave me out of this," I stated, not wanting to get involved.

"Why not? Do you agree?" Lily shot at me and I opened my mouth in shock.

"What? No, well, maybe..."

"Unbelievable!" Lily stood straight up and started crossing her arms. "How long have you two been feeling this way?"

"It doesn't matter!" Mom said firmly and stood up next to her. "It's just hard seeing you like this, Lil. You're so unhappy and everyone can see it. We just want you to feel better. If you love Jake, then dang it, go after him! But if you guys both agreed to break it off, then it's time to move on and find some happiness."

"I don't want to go after him. If he wants me, he knows where to find me. It's not like I've moved or changed my number!" Lily boomed and started pacing the living room.

"Well, then if that's what you want to do, sweetheart," she said warily. Clearly, that was not the answer she was hoping Lily would provide.

"I do. You're right, I just need to be happy and move on. I can do that. I don't need a man in my life to make me happy! I am a strong, independent, confident woman who doesn't need a man by her side! I can do just fine on my own!" she rattled on.

"That's right, you are!" Mom encouraged her.

"If Jake really loved me, he would be here, right now. But since he's not, I'm not going to waste my time hoping he's going to call me or show up! He's not worth my time! I have other things to do with my life and I'm not going to waste it waiting around for someone who's able to throw me away so easily," Lily continued.

"You go, girl!" I teased and my mom shot me a look that said, "really?".

"I *can* do this!" she said again.

"Yes, you can! Now, go take a shower and wash your hair." Mom pointed up the stairs, in the direction of the bathroom and Lily looked caught off guard.

"Wait, what?" she asked, puzzled.

"Girl, I know you haven't washed your hair properly in a while, so go take a nice, long hot shower," Mom said.

"Lather, rinse and repeat," I snickered and this time they both shot me looks.

"Really, you're not helping," she hissed and Lily snorted.

"It's okay, Mom." Lily waved me off. "She's only trying to lighten the mood. I will go shower. Happy?"

"Extremely," she smiled and watched Lily walk up the stairs. Once she was out of sight, my mom turned to look at me. "Couldn't you have said anything to back me up?" she asked flatly and sat back down on the couch next to me.

"No, Mom. She didn't need us to team up on her. That's the last thing she needs she needs to know that we love her and are here for her. Not that I didn't agree with you; she definitely has to stop all the moping and looking like a homeless person. But I didn't want to make her feel uncomfortable," I explained.

"You just wanted me to be the bad guy, so you could look good," she declared.

"Well, that was just a plus," I shrugged and chuckled.

"You're a brat," she pointed out. "I'm glad she's decided to move on. Although, I'm not going to lie, I thought she was going to go after Jake. She's stronger than I gave her credit for. But, now, it's time for her to stop wasting her time on him. Did she ever tell you what happened?"

I shook my head. "No. She just said that there was a misunderstanding and things were said in the heat of the moment, and I guess they both took it to heart."

"She hasn't told me anything either. I guess it wouldn't matter if she did, because actions speak louder than words." I watched her brow slowly furrow, deep in thought.

"After four years though, I just don't get it. There's a piece of the puzzle missing."

"Well, Mom, it's going to be up to them to find it. If they want too. But it sounds like they put the puzzle back in the box, and gave up."

"Aren't you clever?" she quipped and stood to walk into the kitchen.

I laughed and followed her to find some popcorn to snack on.

Lily came downstairs about an hour later, looking refreshed and much happier. She was practically skipping into the kitchen and hijacked my popcorn.

"Feeling better, sis?" I asked and took my popcorn back as she was stuffing a handful in her mouth.

"Yes, actually, much better. I should have done that weeks ago. I think I'm going to head back to the apartment. Susie and Kylee are wanting to meet up tonight and go out to eat with a big group," she said confidently and proceeded to take my popcorn yet again.

"Wow, look at you getting back into it. Who's all going?" I decided to surrender and just take a handful of popcorn out of the bag. The last thing I wanted to do was sweep up an entire bag of popcorn off the floor.

"I think it's Susie's boyfriend, a boy Kylee likes, and some other people. I'm not really sure. They just invited me," she explained and started eating one piece of popcorn at time, just to annoy me.

"Good for you, Lily… you'll have fun. Plus, I bet your friends have missed you," our Mom said and ended the war by grabbing the popcorn and putting it away.

"I'll head back with you. I have a test tomorrow to study for in chemistry. That class is giving me a run for my money. I would rather write an essay any day than try to figure out chemical reactions," I reckoned.

I walked over by Mom, and gave her a hug. "Love you, Mom. Did you want me to close for you on Monday?"

"Yes, I do. I signed up for a painting class with some girls from work," she informed me and I was immediately jealous.

"I want to go to a paint class! Never mind, have Lily close." I tried to shove the shift onto my sister, who immediately started shaking her head.

"No way! I have a test on Tuesday and was planning to study

Monday night. It's all you, Rosie. You can have fun closing with Brad!"

"Wait, what?" I shrieked. "Brad? The freshmen who wouldn't stop eating the cookie dough and ended up getting sick? And who thought washing his hands with just water was good enough?"

"Hey, Brad has come a long way!" my mom stated in his defense. "He's doing much better now, and refuses to actually make the cookie dough now, because of that little incident," she divulged. "Besides, he called in and said he couldn't come in, because he has the same test Lily has on Tuesday. So, I put Troy on instead to close with you."

"Yes!" I said cheerfully. "Troy rocks."

"Oh, lucky!" Lily was clearly bummed out. "That guy is hilarious! He's the best employee! I actually have him in my biology class and he's a crack up. You should have heard him when we were studying the human body. I was practically rolling on the floor, I was laughing so hard." Lily started laughing at the memory.

"Sucker!" I teased. "Monday is going to be fun, not to mention he's fast at closing, so we'll be out of there in no time!"

"Especially since Brad is closing with you on Tuesday night, Lily," Mom informed her and I started snickering while I watched Lily's eyes grow twice their size and her mouth gape.

"No way! I am *not* closing with him! You did that on purpose!" she accused our mother.

At this point, I was laughing so hard, I was bending over, clutching my stomach. It was the funniest thing I had heard all day, although Lily thought this wasn't very nice and attempted to push me over.

"Now, now girls. Lily, I'm closing with you that night, so don't worry. He needs a little more guidance before I let him close without me. You would end up locking him in the bathroom," she joked.

"Listen…" Lily began, but instead shrugged. "Yeah, you're

probably right. At least I'm closing with you, so that doesn't make it near as bad. Where are you going to be, Rosie?"

"I was planning on going grocery shopping, since *someone* has been eating all the food, and has hardly refused to leave the apartment except go to school," I hinted and Lily's head shrunk back.

"Oh, yeah, we're out of a lot of things. Will you grab some more yogurt? I may have eaten all of yours." She started walking quickly out the door, in a poor attempt to run away.

"Are you kidding me? I just bought those a couple days ago. Is that all you've been eating?" I called after her and heard Mom chuckling behind me.

"I sure do miss you girls when you're gone." She kissed my cheek. "You better run after her or she'll leave you."

"She'll be the death of me," I mumbled and followed my rotten sister out the door.

CHAPTER 3

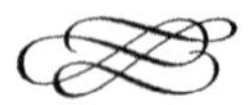

Lily left the house shortly after we got home to run off with her friends, which allowed me to study in peace and quiet. After talking with Mom, we decided she seemed to be doing a lot better and realized she had been wasting time moping. She was a little hesitant leaving the house and had a hard time deciding what to wear, but once Susie and Kylee arrived, she put on a happy face and went on her way.

I managed to finish all my studying and got caught up on my homework, so that I wasn't totally swamped during the rest of the week.

The next day, I took my test and thanks to my partner, I was able to pass the lab portion. I couldn't wait to finish this semester, so I never had to do another science class again. The rest of the day flew by and I was able to stay caught up on my studying for my other classes. I figured my sister was at the house, because that's where she preferred to study, so I hung out in the library. Once I decided my brain had had enough, I headed over to the bakery to meet Troy.

"What's up, Rosie?" he greeted merrily when I walked into the bakery.

"Hi, Troy!" I said excitedly and waved like a little school girl.

The bakery was a small little shop, with tons of character. My mom loved the color pink, so the walls were striped with thick light pink and white stripes. There were a couple sets of hot pink tables and chairs, big enough to seat three people and a huge window that offered different flavored cupcakes, cookies and sweet rolls.

Today, she was featuring five different cupcakes: lime-coconut, dark-chocolate raspberry, lemon-blueberry, vanilla, vanilla-and-chocolate Oreo. Also available were snickerdoodles and chocolate chip cookies and orange rolls. She liked to throw in a pastry every now and again to mix it up. She also had a huge book of cakes that she had previously put together that sat on the counter, so people could get ideas for their own cakes.

She loved to make cakes. She loved that no custom cake was ever the same, unless the customer ordered that. Behind the counter was a huge board that listed all the prices and in the back was where endless amounts of sugar, flour and other ingredients could be found. She also had my favorite twenty-quart mixer back there, where I could knock out dozens of cookies in no time.

I walked around the counter and gave Troy a big hug. "Hey, long time no see! How was Costa Rica?"

Troy had been studying abroad in Costa Rica for school and had been gone for an entire semester. My mom was stoked to hear that he was back and wanted to continue working for her.

"Oh, man, it was amazing! It was gorgeous and I was able to pick up a ton of Spanish. How have you been?"

I pulled out a pink apron, and tied it around my waist, "I've been good. Just trying to keep up on school work and maintain my scholarship. Chemistry is kicking my butt."

"I hear that class is no fun. I dread taking it. Listen, did I hear that Jake and Lily broke up?" he asked quietly.

"Yep, they broke up about three weeks ago," I nodded and started taking inventory of everything.

"Holy crap. I didn't think they were ever going to break up!

Those two seemed perfect for each other." He followed me around while I did inventory. There wasn't much for him to do at night until we closed, because everything was already made and prepped.

"I didn't think so either. They were on some special date last weekend and when I came back home, Lily was crying on the couch and told me they broke up. I could hardly believe it. I thought he was going to propose."

"Oh, man, is she okay?"

"Yeah, I think she's doing a lot better now." I smiled appreciatively "Thanks for asking, Troy. That's very nice of you to be concerned."

"Well, I saw Jake the other night with some other chick and I was really confused. I figured that maybe they were just hanging out as friends, but..." He shook his head. "Never mind."

"Tell me."

"No, you don't want to know." Troy waved it off. "Just know he's a jerk, and I should have punched him when I saw him."

"Troy, tell me now," I pressed and crossed my arms, still holding the clipboard.

"I saw him and this girl kissing," he divulged softly. "I was so confused. I didn't know what to do. I figured I would wait to see you and ask what happened. I should have punched him then and there."

"It's okay, Troy. Probably a good thing that you didn't punch him. It sounds like it was a mutual thing, I think. Although, it sounds like Jake was more okay with the break up than Lily." I uncrossed my arms and began counting the amount of chocolate chips we had. When I found an opened bag of milk chocolate chips, Troy nabbed them out of my hands.

"I'll say. You date someone for four years, and not a month after, he's already sucking face with another woman? Not cool!" grunted Troy and he started eating chocolate chips.

"No, it's not. Lily deserves much better than Jake, if that's how he's acting. And let's just keep this between us, okay? I would hate for her to hear this. She's just barely getting over the breakup… I feel like this would set her back emotionally." I took the chocolate chips back from him.

"Hey! I'm stress-eating!" he joked and tried to take them back.

What was up with people taking things out of my hands lately?I laughed. "How about a cookie? I have a feeling we're going to have a little extra. You can even have two, if you want." I draped an arm around his waist.

"Yeah, two cookies sound good. Three would be better," he grinned and I pushed him playfully.

We laughed and, just as he was about to take a bite of a snickerdoodle cookie, two giggly girls came in; he shot me a pouty look and hid his cookie so no one would take it. In a split second, he turned his frown upside down and greeted the girls like nothing had happened.

"Welcome, ladies. Are you looking for something sweet?" he smiled, flashing his teeth and the two girls blushed and nodded, still giggling.

This was another reason why my mom had hired Troy; he was a handsome, good-humored, hard-working guy, and he attracted the ladies. She was convinced that he sold the most inventory just from his good looks.

He had a surfer look to him, with tanned skin that I assumed he had gotten from Costa Rica, and sandy-blonde hair, and intense blue eyes. In fact, I'm pretty sure he'd told me that he did like to surf. Of average height, Troy had a lean build and a very playful smile. He looked like someone who was up to doing anything and would have a fun time doing it.

I laughed at the flirty girls and went into the back room to finish the inventory. Mom had texted me earlier that day that she wanted me to do some shopping for the bakery too, since I had already planned on going. This meant that my list was growing even longer, but it also committed me to not have to close tomorrow, and Lily couldn't get out of it. Technically, I was still on the clock but, thankfully in a different way, without Brad.

While I was in the refrigerator counting butter and eggs, I heard the bell ring, which didn't faze me, because I knew Troy would be up front to grab the customer. But then, not a moment later, he found me in the fridge and informed me that there was a customer wanting to do a custom order.

Mom had instructed the staff that the only people able to take custom orders were her, Lily and myself. She didn't want to risk someone messing up the order and, as a result, Mom making something the customer wouldn't want. Custom orders were the big money maker and she wanted everything to be done right.

I followed Troy to the front and saw that there was a tall man standing behind the counter, looking at the cupcakes. He was wearing a grey suit, white shirt and dark blue tie, which brought out his dark blue, brooding eyes. He had dark hair, that was gelled and swept to the side… and did I mention drop-dead gorgeous? His jaw was squared with a cleft in the chin. He was definitely a dreamy Prince Charming.

I could feel my cheeks flush and I knew I shouldn't be the one to take care of this customer. I wanted to run the other way and let Troy handle this one, but I figured that wouldn't set a very good example. Plus, he would never let me live it down.

I cleared my throat and tried to speak, but no words came out.

Unfortunately for me, the man heard me clear my throat and he looked up and smiled, "Hi."

"Hi, welcome to Karen's Kreations. What can I help you with?" The line sounded so rehearsed, I felt like I was talking through a drive-through speaker phone. In my mind, I was kicking myself and I could see Troy smiling out of the corner of my eye. He was so going to give me a hard time for this.

"Well, I'm actually waiting for someone, but we need to order a cake for an event. Do you have a flyer where I can see the costs for the size, flavor, design, and whatnot?" He waved his phone around while he was talking. It made him look like an important business man who had things to do, but he was nice and not pushy.

"Yep, Troy, would you mind getting that from under the counter and handing it to him? I need to run to the back really quick, and I'll be right with you, Mr....?"

"Oh, call me Nick."

I smiled. "Okay, Nick, I'll be right with you," I repeated and turned around to hide in the refrigerator.

A couple of minutes later, the refrigerator door opened, and Troy walked in to join me.

"Rosie, what are you doing?" he asked and raised an eyebrow.

"I just needed to finish this last bit of inventory and then I'll be out there to help the customer," I explained and Troy started laughing.

"You're so full of it!" he called out and I opened my mouth in shock.

"What are you talking about?" I tried to play it as cool as possible. "I really *do* have to check how much stock we have, so I know what to shop for tomorrow."

"Oh, bologna!" he cut me off. "I haven't seen you that caught off guard with a customer since that one lady demanded a chocolate cake be made and delivered within an hour of an event. And even then, you handled it better than that!" He gestured to the front and started laughing. "Do you think he's cute, Rose?"

I could feel my face burn up and rolled my eyes. "No! I was just d-distracted and lost my tr-train of t-thought," I stammered and Troy started laughing even harder.

"Oh, man, you *totally* have the hots for him. Should I tell him? Should I say something? Let him know your single?" He chuckled and winked.

"No! Don't you dare!" Before I could say anything more, the

bell for the front door rang and we both immediately left the refrigerator and returned to the front.

In the waiting area, was an exotic tall, thin woman with thick dark brown hair. She looked like she could be an actress in Bollywood, she was so beautiful. She walked over to Nick and gave him a kiss on the cheek, while holding a phone in her hand. She was wearing a ruby-red blazer with a black pencil skirt to show off extremely long legs, and black stilettos to complete the entire look. I could've sworn she just came out of a business meeting. She immediately made me feel like a two-foot tall ragamuffin.

They walked up to the counter together and I put on the best smile possible. "Hi, how can I help you?"

Troy stood to the side of me, wiping down the counters, appearing to be busy, but I knew he was eavesdropping.

"Hello, my name is Alisha," she said with an Indian accent. "We are wanting to order a cake for our wedding in three months. Do you have any availability for June sixth?" she asked while flipping her hair back over her shoulder.

I could physically feel my heart sink to the floor. He was taken. There was no way I could entertain any thoughts with this guy. He was practically a married man. Trying to hide my disappointment, I forced a smile on my face and looked at the happy couple. My mind might know that Nick was with someone else, but my heart sure didn't. When I looked at Nick, I noticed he had been staring at me, smiling. All of a sudden, I realized that I had to focus on my breathing and make sure I was getting oxygen.

"Let me check the calendar." I reached under the counter for it and flipped forward to June, silently praying that it would be filled, but to my dismay, it was completely wide open. "Looks like we have that weekend available. Would you like to set up a cake testing?"

"Yes, that would be perfect. How about Thursday? Will that be enough time?" she inquired.

"Yup," I said shakily. "That should be enough time."

"Perfect. I want to try the white cake with vanilla frosting, the chocolate cake with chocolate frosting, the white cake with raspberry filling and vanilla frosting, lemon cake with lemon frosting, the chocolate cake with strawberry frosting and strawberry filling, and the carrot cake with cream cheese frosting. Did you get all that written down?" she snapped.

"Yup." I read back her cake requests.

"Perfect. We'll be here at six o'clock on Thursday," she informed me and smiled. "Thanks so much." She spun and walked out the front door.

"Thank you," Nick smiled. "It was nice to meet you." He followed his fiancé out the door.

"No, thank *you*," I murmured and penciled in my new favorite customer.

SNICKERDOODLE RECIPE

½ cup softened, salted butter
½ cup vegetable shortening
1 ½ cup sugar
2 room temperature eggs
1 tsp. vanilla
2 ¾ cup all-purpose flour
2 tsps. cream of tartar
1 tsp. baking soda
¼ tsp. salt
¼ cup extra sugar
2 tsps. cinnamon

1. Preheat oven to 350 degrees.
2. Cream together salted butter, vegetable shortening, and sugar until light and fluffy.
3. Add in room temperature eggs and vanilla until fully mixed.

4. Add cream of tartar, salt, baking soda and flour, and mix until incorporated. Do not over mix.
5. Mix extra sugar and cinnamon into separate bowl.
6. Form dough into 1″ balls and press dough into cinnamon sugar on one side. Place cookies, cinnamon sugar side up, on cookie tray.
7. Bake for 10 minutes. Enjoy!

CHAPTER 4

"Well, she was a treat, wasn't she?" Troy asked, but I remained silent and continued writing the order. "Are you okay?" he asked as he strolled to stand alongside me.

"Yeah, why wouldn't I be?" I shrugged.

He put an arm around me and I leaned my head into him. "I'm sorry," he whispered into my hair.

"It's fine. It's no big deal. I just thought he was cute. Whatever. We should get ready to start closing though."

The rest of the night was slow. It made closing really easy, and we were able to leave a little early, which I was grateful for. On my way home, I called my mom to let her know about the cake testing and she was over the moon. She loved making wedding cakes and being able to be a part of someone else's special day. However, when she asked me to help with the tasting, I started to protest.

"Mom, can't you have Lily help you? I did the last cake testing."

"After working with Ben, she's not going to want to do a cake testing. Plus, if the bride sounds as snotty as you described her, she's not going to touch that with a ten-foot pole. Besides, I thought you liked doing weddings?" she questioned.

"I just thought I might let Lily have the chance, that's all. Plus, I've been working a lot and wanted to have a night off." I tried making up a good enough excuse for her to let me off the hook, but I knew she wasn't going to let me.

"Lily just told me that she has a couple tests on Friday and that she needed Thursday to study. I'm sorry, honey, I'm going to need your help. You can have the rest of the weekend off if you like," she offered, sounding a little guilty.

She never wanted to force us to work and treat us like actual employees. She knew that most of the time, we worked to help her out, even though she still paid us. But I needed to get over myself and this little crush, and help Mom. I knew she wouldn't have asked if she didn't really need it.

"Okay, Mom, I can do that. I'll help you. But only if you get Troy to help that night too! He was a blast to work with today," I countered and she laughed.

"Alright, I'll make sure to let him know I'm having him work Thursday. Thanks for closing tonight, honey. I had so much fun painting at tonight's class! We will have to do it one of these weeks, when Lily can close. Have a good night. Love you!"

"Love you too." I ended the call. "She's going to be the death of me," I whispered to myself and continued driving home.

When I walked in, I found Lily and her friends, Susie and Kylee, sitting on the couch, watching a movie.

"Oh, hey sis, how are you doing?" Lily asked.

"Good. I booked a cake testing today for a potential wedding cake in June." I pulled a cup out of the cupboard and filled it with water.

"I bet Mom was excited about it. She loves making wedding cakes." She put a chip in her mouth.

"Yeah, she definitely was. The bride seems like a piece of work though. I'm not excited about it," I admitted and took a sip of water. "What are you ladies up to? I thought you had some studying to do?"

"I did, but my brain started feeling like it was turning to

mush, so I had to take a break," Lily explained, eating another chip.

"She really only studied for like an hour, and then gave up," Susie declared.

"That sounds familiar," I laughed. "How do you expect to pass any of your classes if you don't study?"

"It's called flying by the seat of you pants," Kylee chuckled and took the chip bag from Lily.

"Yup, she's going to try and study as little as possible and get by doing hardly any studying," Susie said and took a handful of chips.

"Whatever!" Lily cried, "I study enough. If I study too much, I just get confused. I have to take breaks!"

"Studying for one hour and then spending the rest of the evening laying around is not a break." Kylee chuckled and handed the chip bag back to Lily. "It's a good thing I study before I hang out with you; otherwise I would never graduate college."

"Are you saying I'm a bad influence?"

"Oh, no," Susie cut in. "We wouldn't say that. You're just so much fun to be around, we would rather hang with you than study."

"Yeah, we knew you would distract us anyways, so we try to plan our study time earlier, before we see you. I mean, seriously, can you blame us? You're cute, bubbly and hilarious." Kylee offered a silly smile.

"You guys are so full of it," Lily sniffed and the three of us started laughing.

"Come on, sis, we know you don't like to study or do homework. It's not a bad thing; no one actually enjoys it. Can you blame Kylee and Susie for doing it before they come over?" I tried to console my overworked sister, who I thought was being way too dramatic.

"I guess not. I would just rather hang out with friends and have fun than study boring old lectures," admitted Lily and started cooling down.

"That's what I thought. Now, on a serious note, are you sure you're ready for your test tomorrow? Don't you think you should study a little more?" I asked cautiously, knowing she was emotional.

"Ugh, fine." Lily picked up the remote and turned off the movie. "I'll study some more."

"And, on that note, I think we should leave." Susie stood and Kylee rose, hovering behind her.

"Agreed. I don't want to study any more than I have to." Kylee yawned and followed Susie out the door.

"Your guys are so helpful," said Lily sarcastically.

"That's why you love us," Susie sang and waved.

"And why you'll never get rid of us," Kylee chimed in.

"Yeah, yeah, yeah." Lily waved them off. "Goodnight, jerks."

"Goodnight!" they replied and shut the door behind them.

I chuckled. "I always forget how much I like those two."

"Yeah, they're real fun to have around," she muttered acerbically.

"Oh, come on, Lil. You know you need to study and you should have gotten it done earlier. Otherwise, you should have just worked tonight. Troy was a blast. He definitely made the night go by fast. Now, you have to study late and work with Brad tomorrow. Lucky you." I smiled and kicked off my shoes.

"You know, sometimes you're not very nice," Lily stated flatly and opened her laptop.

"I never said I was," I replied and walked into my room.

I took off my clothes that smelled like frosting and cookies, put on old gym shorts and a baggy shirt, and laid down on my bed. I thought about Nick and how kind he seemed. His smile was so easy and effortless, it brightened up the whole room. He was the most handsome man I had ever met. Then, once his bride walked in, I couldn't help but wonder why in the world he would want to marry a "brat" like her. I mean, I had heard opposites attract... but not to that extreme. I couldn't imagine working with a bride like that and, quite frankly I had no desire to do so.

I was going to need all the strength I could muster to try and get through their cake testing... and prayed she wouldn't like our cakes.

CHAPTER 5

The next day, I went to the grocery store just as I had planned. Since we had the cake tasting in a couple of days, I had to make sure I had plenty of ingredients to make the order. That was on top of getting our normal stock back up to the usual quantities, and adding my own grocery shopping to the list, I had a lot to buy.

I was tempted to call my mom and see if she wanted to come with me, but I knew if I did that, Lily would throw an absolute fit and refuse to be alone with Brad. Despite Mom being there for moral support more than anything else, I knew Lily was going to be cranky when she got home, so I made a mental note to grab bags of chips for her. I felt like a complete enabler, so I grabbed banana chips too to see if maybe she would attempt a healthier option. However, I knew the likelihood of that was very small.

My sister had the metabolism of a sixteen-year old boy. She was much skinnier than I was, but no one would ever guess that she was skinny by how she ate. She ate donuts and muffins for breakfast, lots of carbs for lunch that consisted of big sandwiches or pizza, and when got home, she would eat lots and lots of chips. The only time she would ever eat healthy was when someone else would cook it for her, which meant me. I insisted on her eating something of substance, so I tried to feed her lots of vegetables and lean proteins for dinner.

The first few weeks of me deciding to take initiative for her poor eating habits, she realized what I was doing and complained about the food I was making. She would insist that it would be easier to order take-out and that vegetables didn't taste good. However, when I began to scare her with the idea of diabetes, she shut up and ate what I made.

Me, I've always had to work for my figure. Growing up working in the bakery, I definitely went through a chubby phase. Then, in high school, I realized that I didn't want to be fat and have poor eating habits. I knew that if I wanted to be a baker for the rest of my life, I needed to find a healthy balance. So, I started counting my calories, tried to eat vegetables at every meal and limited myself to only a couple treats a week. Not only that, but I convinced my mom to let me run track. I wasn't the fastest by any means, but the running and consistent training helped dump the weight. Even now, I tried to get a couple runs in a week or hit the school gym once or twice in an attempt to have some muscle tone. But no matter how hard I tried, my sister was always skinnier than I was and there was nothing I could do about it. Genetics were a cruel part of life.

I turned the corner to walk down the aisle with the many chip options and literally ran into a cart that was coming from the opposite direction.

"Oh, I'm so sorry I didn't mean too…" I lost my voice.

The person in front of me came into focus and I realized I was standing in front of Nick, the handsome man I had met the previous night.

"Rosie, right?" He chuckled and leaned onto his cart, smiling ear to ear.

"Right, and you're Nick?" I played dumb, but I don't think he bought it.

"Yeah, fancy bumping into you here. Looks like you have quite the haul."

He eyed my cart; it was practically overflowing from all the items.

"I'm doing some shopping for the bakery, and a little personal shopping," I explained and could feel my cheeks flush.

"Well, that's good. I was worried you were going to put spinach and tomatoes into my cake," he teased and half-smiled.

I laughed and shook my head. "Nope, definitely not. But the raspberries and strawberries are definitely going in there."

"That's good. Hey, now that I see you here, I was actually wondering if I could add another cake request for the tasting?" he asked sheepishly, which I thought was just plain adorable.

"Sure, what would you like to add?" I pulled out my phone to make a note.

"I love mint chocolate. It's one of my favorite combinations, and I would just love to try it...and see if Alisha would like it. She says that mint is 'too playful' for a wedding, but I think it would be a fun flavor to add."

"I love chocolate and mint! Those girl-scout thin mint cookies are my favorite! I could eat a whole box, no problem," I said, quite bubbly.

He started, laughing at my excitement. "Me too! My sister was a girl scout and would bring them home for me." He grinned at the memory. "We would get in so much trouble once my mom found us surrounded by boxes of cookies. She would end up having to buy the extra boxes we ate. In my opinion, they were worth every penny."

"Oh, no doubt. My mom makes a chocolate-mint cupcake that reminds me of the flavor of a thin mint. It's to die for. I'll have to find that recipe and use it for your cake testing. I think you'll love it!" I beamed.

He nodded in approval, "Alright, sounds great! Now, I'm really looking forward to this cake testing."

"Good. Everyone deserves to have their own touch on their wedding cake." I smiled and he smiled back, which sent my heart beating wildly.

We got stuck staring at each other, smiling like goof-balls in the middle of the aisle. We probably looked like idiots.

Someone walked by and Nick was the first to snap out of it. He cleared his throat and placed his hand on the back of his neck. "Well, thank you so much for adding that… I know you already had quite the list."

"It's no problem. Like I said, everyone deserves their own special cake especially on their wedding day." I started feeling stupid for how completely cheesy that sounded.

"I really appreciate it. I guess I'll see you on Thursday then." He beamed and shifted his cart around me.

"See you soon!" I waved.

When he was no longer in sight, I smacked myself on the forehead and put my head on my cart. Man, I sounded so cheesy; I was cheesier than the mozzarella sitting in my cart. He probably thought I was a complete idiot, with a ravenous appetite, given the full cart.

I shook my head. "Who cares? He's taken," I told myself and wrapped up my grocery shopping. Despite leaving with a cartful of food, I never felt so empty after watching him walk away. What was wrong with me?

The last couple of days went way too fast. Mom had me in the bakery getting the cakes and fillings ready for her to assemble Thursday morning. Because of the cake testing, and all the prep work I had to do, I didn't get to study as much as I wanted to, and barely passed my test. But with my mom being busy with her other job, she needed me to help out.

One time, Lily tried baking multiple cakes at once and ended up burning *all* the cakes. She'd gotten much better since then, but my mom still worried about her messing us especially with a huge potential custom order, and a wedding cake at that. Weddings always meant a big payday.

Wednesday night, Mom stopped in to check my progress and tried all the fillings to make sure everything was perfect.

"Mmm, honey, you get better with that strawberry jam every

time," she complimented me. "Someone must have taught you really well." She smiled and tried the raspberry jam.

"Three guesses who." I laughed and watched her swoon playfully over the raspberry jam.

"This is making me want a peanut-butter-and-jelly sandwich. I haven't had dinner yet. Do we have bread somewhere around here?" She looked around the room.

"I don't think we do." I trailed walked into the pantry to see if I could find any. "Sorry, Mom. That's not a bad idea though. We should keep some bread around here."

"Yeah maybe put that on the list for when you go to the store next time. We have peanut butter and jam already here... might as well have bread for when someone is hungry. It's better than munching on cookies all night the way Brad did last night." She shook her head and threw her spoon into the sink.

I giggled at the thought of Lily working with Brad. "How did that go?"

"Well, he messed up five different orders, dropped three cupcakes and then proceeded to eat them off the floor in front of a customer. And, then, he accidentally tripped with a cupcake in his hand and it landed in Lily's hair." She chortled at the memory and went to look at the cakes.

This was sweet music to my ears and I laughed in fact, I laughed so hard, I grabbed the counter for support. "Please tell me you got that on the security camera, because I need to see that, " I cackled. (I wasn't really a mean person, but that sounded like sweet justice to me.)

"Well, your sister didn't think it was very funny. She insisted that she had to go home to shower and left me to close with Brad, which took twice as long as usual, mind you," Mom complained and started putting the cakes and fillings back in the fridge.

"That explains why she was home before me. I asked her how work was, but she didn't say much. She probably didn't want me to find out. Granted, I guess I can't blame Lily, because

I would have given her such a hard time," I admitted and started helping her carry things to the fridge.

"Remember to be easy on your sister. She just went through that hard break-up with Jake. Her heart is a little more tender right now than usual," my mom chided and I rolled my eyes when she couldn't see me.

"Mom, it's been like a month. She seems fine and hasn't had any meltdowns the last week. Plus, I think she's going to a party this weekend with Kylee and Susie."

"Maybe she's just putting on a tough face? We don't know what's going through that girl's mind. I worry about her. I know I wanted her to move on and forget Jake, but a party seems a little fast. Maybe you should go with them," she suggested and I gaped.

"No way. You know I don't party. I hate parties!" I sauntered to the front to see if any of the treats needed to be restocked.

She followed behind and leaned up against the counter. "I know you do, and I don't blame you. I wouldn't go to those college parties if someone paid me, but I need to have an extra set of eyes on her. Just until I know for sure she's over this once and for all."

"Mom, she's twenty; she doesn't need a babysitter anymore," I argued and turned to find a concerned look on her face.

She looked more tired than usual, which didn't make any sense. She had purple bags under her eyes, and her hair was a little messier than usual, like she hadn't washed her hair in several days.

"I know, but it doesn't mean she doesn't need to be looked after. Please consider going," she pleaded with tired, green eyes.

"Fine, I'll consider it, but that doesn't mean yes," I advised and walked to the back room to grab more cupcakes.

"Honey, why don't you go home?" Mom suggested.

"What?" I was confused by her question.

"I know you've been working a lot and I've asked a lot of

you, so why don't I close tonight and you go home and relax?" She took the cupcakes from my hands.

"Are you sure, Mom? I don't mind helping." Now I felt bad for complaining about helping Lily and being frustrated about not having had enough study time for my test.

"Yes, and after the cake tasting tomorrow, I'm giving you the rest of the weekend off," she told me and returned to the front of the bakery.

"Why? I don't mind working, Mom. I like to help you."

"I know you do, sweetie, but I can tell you're tired. I've had you doing stuff everyday this week for the bakery and I still need you here tomorrow. That's a lot. Plus, I'm sure you have some studying to catch up on. Especially if you decide to go to that party with your sister this weekend," she stated with a coy smile.

"You're persistent, *Mother*, I'll give you that. But, you're right. I do have some studying to get caught up on, whether I go to that party or not," I made sure to clarify as I took off my apron.

"Just think about it, love. I'd really appreciate it," she reiterated and pulled me in for a hug. "Thank you for everything you do, Rosie."

"You're welcome, Mom. Love you. And thanks for closing. I really appreciate it. Troy's coming tomorrow for the cake testing, right?" I wanted to make sure I had a little moral support, because Troy knew what had occurred a couple days before.

"Yes, he said he could come in. In fact, when I told him he was going to help out with the cake testing and that you were going to be there, he seemed very eager. Do you know why?" She raised an eyebrow, as if she knew she was on to something.

"I don't know. Maybe he likes seeing people taste cakes? I don't know." I shrugged and headed out the door. "Bye. See you tomorrow."

"Love you. Goodnight!" she called after me.

I was out the door before she could ask any questions I might, or might not, have wanted to answer.

CHAPTER 6

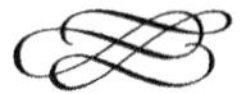

Thanks to my mom, I was able to get caught up on a lot of homework. It also helped that Lily wasn't at the apartment when I came home, so I knocked out a bunch of assignments. I was all caught up and ready for the weekend, unless my teachers decided to throw something else at me in the next two days, which I prayed they didn't.

Lily walked through the front door around ten o'clock, while I was sprawled on the couch, watching Netflix.

"Where have you been?" I asked, genuinely curious. Miss Social Butterfly always had to be hanging around someone doing something.

"Just at Kylee and Susie's. They actually decided to help me through some math problems and then we had a few other friends over and we played games," she told me and tried to walk quickly past.

"Wait, friends as in *boys*?" I called after her and she froze in place.

"Maybe," she squeaked and turned to face me.

"Are these the boys Kylee and Susie are interested in, or you?" I inquired and realized I was smiling drolly.

"Both? I guess. I don't know. We met them yesterday at the

yogurt place, and they seemed like really nice guys and they went to our school... and they invited us to a party this Friday. Then Kylee, being Kylee, invited these boys over to kinda get to know them better before we actually decided to go to this party." Lily's voice had gotten smaller and smaller, to the point where I had to strain to hear the last word.

"Wait, wait, wait. Kylee invited complete strangers to her apartment? Is she crazy?" I shrieked and turned off the TV.

"Yes she did and yes she is," Lily confirmed and stared at her feet.

"You know how dangerous that is? Anything could have happened to you girls tonight. I cannot believe you went over there. You're lucky nothing happened!" I pointed my finger at her and took a deep breath to try and control my anger.

"Rose, will you chill? They seemed like really nice guys and we asked around with some of the other girls in our classes and found out they were indeed nice guys. It's all good. And, while I got you all heated, we did in fact decide to go to the party." She made a smug face at me and turned around and walked into her room.

"You're insane," I retorted and put a pillow on my face.

"I'm doing what you and Mom told me to do, remember? Move on! Find my happiness! Have fun!" She slammed shut the door, as if doing this for dramatic effect.

"You could have a least been a little more careful, and maybe used that big head of yours! Are you sure going to this party is such a good idea? Are a lot of other people you know going to this party? Do you know where it is?"

I waited for her to reappear from her room.

She swung open the door and marched into the living room, stopped by the couch I was sitting on. "Yes, it's a good idea. I told you, I'm ready to move on... and I'm tired of staring at these same walls everyday. I want to have fun. And yes, there's a few people I know going to this party, and you do too. Most of the people I know are students from your class: Brittany, Jessica,

Marvin and Brody. They're all going to be there. Even Troy is going to be there. When's the last time you got out and did something fun, Rose? Are you going to become a hermit and never have a social life? Forgive me if I choose not to do that," she ranted, crossing her arms. "I'm going to this party. I already know Mom asked you to come and keep an eye on me. And I bet I already know what the answer to that was!"

"I'm sorry if I don't feel like babysitting my dramatic, emotional, bratty sister at a party I wasn't invited to and have no desire going to," I shot at her and watched her face turn a few shades redder.

"Suit yourself! Have fun being here all alone this weekend. Mom is catering some event a couple hours outside of town and is taking Monique and Veronica. So, you'll have no one. Just the empty silence of this apartment," she snapped. "I'm going to bed. Goodnight!"

She banged the door behind her. I didn't bother saying goodnight; I was too upset.

She had been completely out of line. Granted, I hadn't been much better and had called her a couple things that weren't necessary, but she'd pushed me. My sister and I didn't argue a whole lot. Sure we bickered and teased each other often we were sisters but fighting didn't usually happen. However, when it did, we usually moved past it pretty quickly. We'd see how long it took us this time.

Thursday finally came and I watched the clock all day. Troy messaged me during my history lecture, wondering if I was mentally prepared to see "Mr. Handsome" tonight. When I read the text, I inadvertently snorted and received a couple of unimpressed glances from fellow classmates.

I responded that there was no need to worry about my mental state and that I was going to be fine. Right after I finished my classes and did some last-minute studying on things I wasn't too confident on, I walked to the bakery. Which was only a few blocks away from the university. It was about four in the afternoon by the time I arrived.

I found my mom scrambling around like a chicken with her head cut off. "Mom, are you okay?"

"I'm just trying to make sure everything is perfect for this cake tasting. I decided to make cute four-inch cakes and decorate them in different ways to give the bride an idea of how I can decorate the wedding cake," she said, grabbing more piping bags.

"So, basically, you've created way more work for yourself than you needed to do," I remarked and put my stuff away in the back.

"Yep, pretty much. But, I really want to nail this tasting. Those wedding cakes bring in a good chunk of change and I have a feeling this could be a big order." She panted softly from running around and started piping on what looked to be the chocolate-strawberry cake.

"Do you need any help, Mom?" I asked tentatively while staring at eight stacked cakes, waiting to be decorated.

"Yes, could you please start piping roses? Some white and blush pink ones, in different sizes. Do some big open ones and a couple buds, and then put them in the blast chiller, so when I'm ready to place them, they're nice and frozen."

"I can do that. When is Troy-" I got cut off by the sound of the bell ringing up front and walked up to see Troy entering. "Speak of the devil."

"Are you talking about me, trouble?" He smiled and gave me a big hug.

"Who are you calling trouble?" I questioned. "If anyone is in trouble, that would be *you*. You're up to no good!"

"You're probably right, but I, at least, am not the one who's totally crushing on the groom," he muttered in my ear and I smacked his arm.

"Shut up, man. My mom is back there." I whispered. "And I

am not crushing on the groom. I simply thought that he was cute, and filled out his suit quite nicely, that's all!"

Troy began laughing and shook his head. "You are totally smitten. Too bad he's taken and is about to get married in three months."

"Troy, is that you?" my mom called from the back.

"Yes, Karen. The one and only!" Troy spread his arms out as he walked into the back.

"Thank heaven," I said quietly and Troy waved at me playfully as I entered the back.

"Has it been busy today up front?" he asked, holding an apron to put on.

"No, not really. I mean, it's been okay, but Thursdays aren't usually busy days, which I've been grateful for, because I've needed to focus on these cakes," my mom said, walking up besides me.

"Wait, did you take off work today?" I asked.

"Kinda, not really. I woke up early to work on things, and then I came into open and start on the cakes… and, then, once I had all the cakes stacked and smoothed out, I put them in the fridge and worked a little more. That way I didn't have to necessarily take a personal day. Will you please start working on those flowers? They're going to be here in less than two hours." She was clearly starting to panic.

"You know," I said, picking up a piping bag, "you've cut it close before, but not like this." I began busting out roses and putting them on a sheet tray.

"I know, I know. I even had you get all the fillings and cakes done. I should have stacked sooner," she groaned while piping.

"It's going to be fine, Mom. We're going to get it done and they're all going to look beautiful. And Nick and Alisha are going to love them, okay?" I said encouragingly.

She took a deep breath and walked away from the cakes to wipe her forehead with the back of her hand. "I know… you're right. I need to relax and keep working, and not complain."

"And lucky for you, you've had years of experience and a steady hand. You can pipe all this out in no time and we all know it's going to look amazing, Karen," Troy said in a more serious tone than his usual playful, happy one as put a hand on her back. "*You got this*!"

"Aw, thanks Troy!" She gave him a one-armed hug, careful not to touch him with her hand.

"Suck up," I coughed and Troy flapped an arm at me, as if he were trying to smack me from a distance.

"Well, I think you're very sweet," my mom said. "At least, someone around here is," she joked and turned her head to look at me.

Troy started busting up, thinking it was the most hilarious joke he had ever heard.

"Y'all are hilarious, really," I said sarcastically and put a full tray of roses into the blast chiller.

Luckily, the sound of the bell summoned Troy to the front and my mother and I were left alone work on the cakes. We worked in silence, anxiously watching the clock tick by. Within the hour, I finished three pans of buttercream roses, and put them in the blast chiller just as she finished doing buttercream lace and piped lattice work on the cakes.

She put the cakes in the fridge for a few minutes to allow the frosting to set and then inspected the roses I'd piped. "You're getting better and better each time, Rosie," she complimented me. "Pretty soon, I won't even need to come into work and you can just do everything."

"Would you really let me do that though? I think you're a little too much of a control freak to do that," I teased and she chuckled in response.

"You're probably right, but I'm serious." She put the buttercream roses back in the freezer and sat down in a chair. "You've done amazing. I think the couple is going to be very impressed."

"Thanks, Mom. I hope so," I breathed deeply and pulled up a chair next to her. "That lady seems like a real treat," I muttered.

I had no desire to see her walk through those doors again. Luckily, my mom was going to be doing most of the talking and I merely had to bring out the cakes and put the fakest smile on my face as possible.

"Oh, honey, don't let her get to you. Plus, you should know that women become crazier when it comes to their weddings. They want everything to be absolutely perfect. Trust me, you'll be the same exact way. Just do me a favor, and don't pick me to do your wedding cake." She laughed merrily and put a hand on my leg. "I'm kidding, sweetheart. You ask someone else and I'll hunt you down. You know how badly I've wanted to make your wedding cake, if you'll ever get married."

"Here it comes," I groaned and leaned back.

"When is the last time you've been on a date? I thought your sister was going to get married before you with Jake, but now that that's over..." She trailed off to gather her thoughts. "No, she'll probably still get married before you."

"What's the big deal, Mom? So, I haven't been on a date for a while and I don't have marriage on the radar, but who cares? I've just been focusing on finishing school and the bakery. Plus, I have enough going on with Lily's drama. I couldn't imagine if I was dating someone too and dealing with that drama." I rolled my eyes, thinking about the previous day when we were fighting. She'd truly been quite the handful.

"Yes, but I feel like you're lonely. I mean, I know you're not depressed or anything, but I just want to know that someday you're going to be loved and taken care of and have a family." My mom leaned forward and looked at me earnestly. "You do a lot for me and your sister, but I worry that you're not putting yourself first enough, if at all. I want you to be happy. I want you to date and fall in love, and focus on yourself for once. But there are times when I seriously worry you're going to end up alone." She stood back up to get out the cakes and roses.

"Mom, I hate having this conversation," I admitted. "I just haven't dated a lot. There hasn't been anyone that has really caught my eye and I guess I haven't really been looking. Lily has dated enough for the both of us."

"Be nice to your sister," she warned. "I know you're focused on other things right now, but could you start opening your eyes a little bit?" She almost sounded as if she were pleading as she began placing roses on the cakes.

I shook my head in disbelief. She had no idea. If she knew I was dreading seeing Nick, because I thought he was Mr. Scrumptious, she would flip and think I was completely insane. I really hadn't dated in years. I had a short-lived boyfriend my junior year, who I caught cheating on me under the bleachers after a soccer game with one of Lily's friends, and went on a couple random dates my freshman year of college. But other than that, it really hadn't been on my mind. I'd been perfectly content going to school, working, and watching romantic movies on Netflix.

"Sure, Mom, I'll keep eyes peeled," I promised as I gazed around the room through half-closed eyes.

She began laughing and shook her head. "Your sarcasm kills me sometimes."

"Yes, but it's who I am." I gave a cheesy smile and stood up to look at the clock. "It's 5:45, Mom. You almost done?"

"Yes, I just need to pipe a couple leaves. You can't make pipe roses and not have leaves," she scoffed.

"That's just not realistic," we said together and Mom made a face at me.

After five minutes of her adding more leaves to the cakes and examining them over and over again, she finally relaxed and smiled. "Alright right, they're done."

"They're beautiful, Mom. They're going to love it," I gushed.

"Thanks, sweetheart. I hope they do."

"Well, we'll find out soon enough, because they're walking in right now," Troy announced and straightened his apron.

I felt my heart immediately start to beat faster, my palms start to sweat and my face flush. I was a mess. "Snap out of it," I told myself. "He's just another customer, so *relax*."

"What's that, honey?" my mom asked as she put the cakes in the fridge to let the buttercream set one last time.

"Nothing." I waved it off. "I'm just talking to myself."

Troy ambled over to me and whispered in my ear, "More like a pep-talk, Rose?"

I hit his chest playfully and he returned to the front, getting ready to greet the happily engaged couple. I decided to go to the bathroom and inspect my appearance.

I quickly brushed my wavy blonde hair and inspected the makeup I had put on from this morning. I usually didn't wear a lot of makeup because I figured I had no one to impress, and I only ever went to three different places, occasionally four: the college, bakery, my apartment, and the grocery store. I didn't see the point of wearing it. Today though, I'd decided it was best to put a little on.

Within seconds of finishing my self-inspection, the bell rang, and I heard Troy's muffled voice say, "Hello! Welcome back to Karen's Kreations!"

CHAPTER 7

I walked out of the bathroom and stood behind the corner, just so I was close enough to hear their conversation clearly, but couldn't me.

"Hey, nice to see you again," I heard Nick say. His voice was velvety and deep, and it made me want to hear it more.

"Yes, hello," Alisha snapped. "Are the cakes ready?"

"They sure are," I heard Mom respond. "How are you two doing today? My name is Karen and I'm the owner of the bakery."

"It's nice to meet you, Karen." Nick spoke again. "My name is Nick and this is my fiancé, Alisha. We are here for the cake testing."

"Wonderful," she said happily. "Why don't you two take a seat at a table and I will bring out the cakes." I heard her clap once and then the sound of her feet drawing closer to me.

I decided to make myself known and stepped from the safety of the corner.

"Oh, there you are!" she said, relieved. "I've been wondering where you were. That man up there, Nick?" She pointed to the front, "He is one good-looking guy; it totally caught me off guard. I actually blanked on what I wanted to say for a second.

You were right about the fiancé though; she's colorful. This should be fun." She offered a positive smile.

"Yeah, well, don't take it personally. It seems she's always like that," I muttered and followed Mom to the fridge.

"Will you grab a couple of the cakes and walk them out please? And then will you grab a knife and a couple plates with forks, please?" she requested and took a couple of the cakes.

"Sure thing, Mom," I responded as Troy entered the fridge.

"Can I help with anything, Karen?" he asked with a smug smile. He was trying to get to me.

"Suck up," I mouthed to him and he stifled a laugh.

"Could you grab a couple cakes for me, Troy? Thank you so much; you are too sweet." My mom adored Troy.

"I just like to help," he stated matter-of-factly, and I proceeded to pretend to vomit behind Mom's back.

Troy snorted and grabbed two cakes, as he was told to, and stuck his tongue out at me. I rolled my eyes in response and we followed my mother to the front where the happy couple was sitting.

I saw Alisha's face light up, a change from her usual pout. Nick's face looked equally impressed and once he saw me, he winked at me. Wait, he winked *at me*.

Troy turned back at me, to see if I had noticed, and I felt myself blush.

We lined the cakes on the table and I immediately turned around to grab the forks and plates. When I came back, I handed them to both Nick and Alisha and sauntered behind the counter to where Troy stood, and watched my mom work her magic.

Troy bent down so that he was near my ear. "Did I really see him wink at you?"

I looked at him and nodded, and he smiled as he shook his head. He bent down to my ear one more time to say just three words: "You are trouble."

I snorted and looked at the table, and noticed that Nick had been staring at us. He must have been watching our interaction and his facial expression almost looked like he was, well, bugged. Alisha was oblivious and didn't notice anything; she was too busy making goo-goo eyes at the cakes.

"These are even better than I thought they would be!" she exclaimed with a classic I'm-going-to-compliment-you but-still-offend-you at the same time. "I absolutely love roses, but instead of buttercream, I would prefer to have gum-paste roses to make them look more life-like. The color palate is perfect, everything for the wedding is going to be a beautiful blush and ivory color. I think my favorite cake is this one, with the edible lace wrapped around it and the top full of flowers. I can imagine that being our cake topper. Don't you, sweetheart?" She turned to Nick, prompting him to return to the present.

" Uh, Yes, it's my favorite too," he agreed and glanced over at me again.

I tried to stay motionless and keep my expression unreadable, but it didn't help that Troy had noticed him looking at me either, and had started hitting my thigh, under the counter.

"You know what, Nicky?"

This is where my blank expression cracked blank and I looked down with a smile, and attempted to maintain my composure. The nickname was too much.

"I love these all so much. I think each technique should be represented somewhere on the cake hand-piping, lattice work, lace, beading, rosettes, stenciling. They should all be there! But I'm confused. Why are there eight cakes here? I thought I only requested seven?"

"Oh, well, my daughter Rosie saw Nick at the grocery store and he requested a chocolate-mint cake. He said it was his favorite and wanted to see it as an option," my mom explained smoothly. My stomach did a nervous flip when I saw Alisha look at me with confusion and annoyance, and then turned to Nick.

Nick, however, appeared calm, cool and collected, like it was no big deal. "I thought it might be a fun addition. Is that okay with you?"

"I guess it doesn't hurt to try out every option," she conceded, but I could tell she didn't care to be out of the loop.

"There's a saying around here that you can never have too much cake," my mom said merrily, trying to cut the tension. "Shall we begin?" She looked at Alisha, awaiting her answer, obviously ensuring that Alisha was still the one in control.

"Yes," she replied curtly.

"Perfect. We will go down the line here. Let's try the good ole' white cake with vanilla buttercream." She pointed to the first cake.

They both inserted their forks into the sides of the cake and took a bite. Immediately, their eyes lit up, and whatever "disagreement" they had had before was no longer reflected on their faces.

"Wow, Karen, that is delicious," she complimented my mother and went in for another bite.

"There is nothing boring about that cake," Nick agreed, which caused Alisha to glance sideways at him.

"Boring? That's what you say about this cake?" she questioned and raised an eyebrow. Surprise, surprise, she was annoyed again.

"I meant no offense. When you have all these really yummy flavors stacked up against a plain vanilla cake, you don't really expect it to knock your socks off, but this is hands-down the best one I've ever had," Nick explained and took another bite.

"Thank you, Nick, that's very kind of you," Mom said politely, trying to ease the discomfort in the room.

"Or something like that," muttered Alisha.

Nick looked over at her, clearly irritated, but didn't say anything. He looked at me for a second, but it was unclear what he was trying to say via his facial expression.

Then Alisha spoke again. "Should we move on?"

"Yes, let's do! The next one is close to the same thing, except it's filled with homemade raspberry jam," my mother explained proudly.

The front door bell rang and a group of young soccer players came in and distracted me from the cake tasting. The noise level was pretty loud, with lots of talking and giggling from the girls, so I couldn't hear anything going on with Nick, Alisha, or my mom.

Troy and I tag-teamed the entire soccer team and made sure to get everyone their preferred treat. The coach came up, clearly exhausted, but happy to pay for his girls. Then they all left, with each girl waving and saying thank you. It had taken about twenty minutes to get through all the girls, so by the time Troy and I turned our attention back to the cake tasting, the couple were almost finished.

"This one is the carrot cake, with cream-cheese frosting." My mom pointed to the second-to-last cake. "I love having this one at Easter." She tried making conversation, but neither one of them took the bait.

"It's delicious but, in a way, I think you're right. This wouldn't be very good for a wedding cake," Alisha determined with a slight frown and put down her fork.

"I think carrot cake can be eaten on all occasions. Especially if it's *this* carrot cake." Nick pointed with his fork and took another bite.

"Well, it's a no from me. Let me guess, the last one is the chocolate mint?" Alisha said sharply and picked up her fork again.

"Yes! I've been waiting to try this one," Nick said excitedly.

"Yes, it is Alisha," my mom confirmed. "It's a chocolate cake with mint-chocolate buttercream and, as a surprise, it has crushed thin mint cookies between the layers. A little birdie told me you loved thin mint cookies and insisted I incorporate them into the cake."

Nick's head snapped up to look at me and gave me a huge smile. I gave him a little smile in return, but it quickly disappeared after seeing Alisha's lips pressing tightly together. I could tell she was not happy with me and that she did not want to try this cake. But she wanted to appear to possess class, so she forked up a small sample.

On the other hand, a very excited Nick got a big forkful of chocolate minty goodness. I couldn't decide which reaction to watch, so I tried to pay attention to both. Nick's eyes sparkled and he appeared pleased with what he had just tasted so much so, he went for another bite as soon as he'd swallowed the first. Alisha looked resentfully at the cake; she had already made up her mind but, once she tasted it, she looked pleasantly surprised.

"Karen! This is my favorite cake, ever. It has everything a mint lover like me could want. Moist chocolate cake, fluffy mint frosting, and a little crunchy texture from the thin mint cookies. It's like a party in my mouth and I love it! This is what I want for the wedding. Everyone is going to love this cake." He turned to Alisha, who appeared indifferent.

She shrugged and pushed the cake away. "I'll admit it's a good cake. But I think I liked the white cake, raspberry filling and vanilla buttercream better. I think that is more suitable for a wedding cake."

"There's no way it could be more suitable, because a wedding, in a way, is a representation of *us*. It's our day and we can do and have whatever we want," Nick pointed out.

Alisha turned her head away from Nick and looked at my poor mother, who looked like the monkey in the middle. "Karen, thank you so much for these beautiful cakes. They're a piece of art and every one of them tasted divine. I think we have some things to consider and we will get back to you next week."

"No problem. Let me grab a box for you to take the rest of these home. Maybe you can have your families help decide and let them get a sneak peak," she offered.

Quickly, I grabbed some boxes from under the counter and handed them to my mother, and watched her box them up.

"I don't think I'll be sharing that chocolate-mint cake," Nick admitted.

"That's fine. I don't think anyone else is going to want it,"

Alisha said tartly, which stopped any further conversation about the chocolate-mint cake. "Karen," Alisha held out her hand, "thank you again, I'll be in touch." She spun around and walked out the door without her fiancé.

"I'm sorry about that, you guys. I didn't mean to put anyone in an uncomfortable situation," Nick apologized, looking guilty.

"Oh, Nick, you didn't," My mom assured him and put her hand lightly on his arm. "One of those cake flavors should have been something *you* wanted to try. It's your wedding too, but that's none of my business. That's between you and Alisha."

"Yeah..." He turned around, looking at the exit. "That's going to be my next hurdle. I really appreciate you guys making these cakes, they were all delicious. It's going to be hard to just choose one."

"You're welcome." My mom walked around and gave him a hug. She was a hugger, which used to bug me, but it was her love language and her way of making people comfortable. It definitely wasn't mine. "You let me know what you two decide, okay? Remember: it's for a happy day and not a day that's meant to be too stressful."

My mom had always offered advice and suggestions, even when they weren't necessarily asked for. Luckily, she usually came off as thoughtful and kind, so she didn't usually get in trouble for offering opinions.

"Thank you, Karen." He hugged her back and picked up the cake boxes. "We will definitely let you know what we decide."

"Have a good day, Nick." She waved.

"You too, Karen. Bye, Rosie." He smiled at me and then nodded in Troy's direction as a way of saying goodbye.

"See you later." I watched him leave the bakery.

"Well, that was awkward," Troy stated and I nodded in agreement.

Nick and Alisha were clearly at odds, and didn't seem to care how they were coming off to complete strangers. It made me wonder how they acted toward each other when they were alone. I couldn't imagine the two of them being that happy… certainly not happy enough to get married and spend a lifetime together.

"Those are two people who want completely different things. In marriages, you have to compromise and, when one person is unwilling to, it makes it hard." Sighing, my mother continued, "Having different opinions is a good thing. You still want to be your own person, but being *too* different can make things harder than it should be. It makes you wonder whether it will last… and if you love that person enough to be willing to do anything to stick through to the end. I see so many couples come in here asking for wedding cakes, so I get to interact and observe quite a bit. Some are obviously more in love than others. It's hard to see the ones that aren't as in love, because deep down, you know the likelihood of it working is not great."

She finished her speech and walked to the back of the bakery to clean up. She was clearly not referring to other couples and their potential marriages, but had been thinking about her own past. It was hard to see her still upset from her past decisions and even now dealing with them internally.

I looked at Troy who was giving me a funny look. "What?" I asked suspiciously.

"Your mom made a move faster than you did," he laughed.

"I was never going to make a move," I replied. "He's about to get married and loves Alisha."

"Did you see the way he was looking at you?" Troy exclaimed.

"Yeah, I saw that wink," Mom said upon returning to clean up the table where they had been sitting.

"Mom," I groaned, but she held up a hand.

"It doesn't matter. He's getting married, so let's stop talking about it. He was probably just being friendly anyway," she decided.

After my mom finished cleaning everything up, she left Troy

and me to close up for the night; this left time for me and Troy to talk alone.

"Well, that was an interesting evening don't you think?" Troy asked, wiping down the counters.

"Yep, definitely one for the books," I agreed.

"I swear, I felt a chill down my spine when Alisha walked in," he admitted and started emptying the case from the leftover cupcakes.

I snorted. "She doesn't have the happiest presence, does she?"

"I don't know how Nick puts up with it. She was being completely rude and demoralizing to him in front of complete strangers. Can you imagine how mean she is to him when they *aren't* around people?"

"But he has to know what he's getting himself into. He did propose to her, after all."

"Maybe he didn't realize it? Plus, he thinks he's in love with this girl. If he was so in love with her, why does he have wandering eyes?" Troy asked.

"Don't you think that's a little worrisome? Even if somehow, magically, it worked out with us... what if he had wandering eyes while we were together... toward someone else?" I countered and started mopping the floors.

"Or maybe he has wandering eyes because he's beginning to realize he's with a crazy, angry woman? We have no idea. I just hope he realizes it soon, because no one wants to be married to that. She didn't even want him to have a cake he liked, just to try."

"Maybe there's more to her than her being a control freak? Maybe he's seen the good in her and loves her for it?"

"Rosie." Troy took a deep breath. "Maybe he's starting to be a little realistic and realizes that when he gets married, he marries the good, the bad and the ugly?"

I opened my mouth to argue, but what was the use? He had made a good point and I didn't have a leg to stand on. There was definitely the "good, bad and ugly" floating around in that relationship and they were going to have to figure it out. I held my hands up in surrender,

Troy did a fist pump in the air.

I chuckled, rolling my eyes, and started wiping down all the surfaces, making sure the bakery was prepped for the morning shift.

That was easily the most awkward cake testing I had ever witnessed, and I had done most of them with Mom. If there was that much tension between the two of them concerning the wedding, did they really know what they were doing? Or were love blinders playing a major role? Was it terrible that I was getting my hopes up… just a little bit?

CHOCOLATE CAKE RECIPE

3 cups white sugar
3 cups all-purpose flour
1 ½ cups cocoa powder
1 tbsp. baking soda
1 ½ tsps. baking powder
1 ½ tsps. salt
4 room temperature eggs
1 ½ cups room temperature buttermilk (can be substituted with 1 ½ cups milk and 1 tbsp. of lemon juice or vinegar but let it sit 10 minutes before using)
1 ½ cups hot water
½ cup oil
2 tsps. vanilla extract

1. Mix together sugar, flour, cocoa powder, baking soda, baking powder and salt.
2. Add in eggs, buttermilk, hot water, oil and vanilla and mix until just combined.

3. Separate batter into three 8″ pans. Takes about three cups of batter in each pan.
4. Bake for about 35 minutes. Test with toothpick in the center of the cakes and see if it comes out clean.
5. After about 5-10 minutes, turn out the cakes and cool on a wire rack until cool.
6. Stack and frost the cake with buttercream frosting provided below, or with your favorite frosting!

CHOCOLATE BUTTERCREAM FROSTING

1 cup softened butter
4 1/2 cups sifted powdered sugar
4 tbsps. cocoa
1 tsp. vanilla
2 tbsps. heavy cream
3-4 tbsps. milk

1. Cream together softened butter, until fluffy.
2. Add in powdered sugar and cocoa until mixed together.
3. Mix in vanilla and heavy cream.
4. Slowly add in milk. Do not add all the milk at the same time or else your frosting will separate. Continue adding milk until the frosting is smooth and creamy.

CHAPTER 8

The next day, Mom received a phone call from Alisha, saying that she wanted her to make the wedding cake. They set an appointment at the following week to meet about the details of the cake, and Alisha made sure to note that Nick would not be coming. Apparently, he didn't care what the cake looked like, he just wanted to make sure the cake tasted good. I guess that meant the cake wasn't going to be much of a representation of the wedding couple, and just Alisha. I was beginning to think this was going to be the theme of the entire wedding.

After school, I came home to find my sister in the bathroom getting ready for the party. I stood in the doorway and watched her put on makeup.

"Should we make up now, or stay upset a couple more days?" I teased and waited for her to respond.

"I don't think I'm ready to forgive you yet," she said tartly and continued applying foundation to her already pretty face.

"What if I told you I decided to come to that party?" I asked and she stopped applying her makeup.

"Are you serious?"

I shrugged, pretending to be very interested in my fingernails. "Why not? I have nothing better to do. I could stay home and binge watch some major *Gilmore Girls*, or I could watch you go crazy at some party. And since I've had my fill of *Gilmore Girls* this week, I decided going to this party wouldn't be quite so bad. Besides, I have a couple of tests on Monday and I can't go to Mom's this weekend, so I can't get too distracted. I need to spend most of my weekend locked up in this apartment. But spending an hour or two, giving my brain a break to watch people act like idiots, shouldn't hinder my test-taking performance too much."

"Does Mom know you're going?" she asked, fully turning her attention on me. She stared at me in awe, not fully processing what I was saying. I don't think she completely believed me when I said I was going to the party.

"Yes. When she called me and told me Alisha wanted her to make the wedding cake, I decided that I was going to go to the party. Plus, she had told me she wanted me to think about going. You know, to keep an eye on you and to get out there more, and meet new people. I simply told her that I had thought about it and decided to go," I explained to my little sister, who was still gaping. "Lily, relax. I'm not staying for very long."

"I don't care that you're coming, I just can't believe you are coming. This is crazy. What brought this on? I don't think you've ever been to a party..." She trailed off, trying to recall if I had ever gone.

She would undoubtedly come to the conclusion that I never had; I personally thought they were a waste of time, but clearly I was alone in this opinion.

"No, I haven't. And just because I'm going to this one, doesn't mean I'm always going to go. I'm just trying something new. That's all," I insisted and walked into my bedroom to pick out something to wear.

This time, Lily walked into my doorway and stood there watching me go through my closet. "Troy told me about the cake testing," she said smugly. I guess this was her way of forgiving me.

"Oh, yeah?" I tried to play it cool. "What did he tell you?"

"That the groom is totally into you," she giggled and walked in and laid on my bed. "Tell me about him. Is he handsome? Dreamy? Rich? Successful? Smart? Athletic? Ripped?"

"Lily, relax. I don't really know much about the guy. Well, I guess I do know that he is handsome. I guess I would say dreamy and, from the looks of it, yeah, he's packing some muscle." I held up a leather jacket and a jean jacket, trying to decide between the two.

"The jean jacket. Wear it with your black skinny jeans and grey booties," Lily said, bossing me around.

Instead of arguing, I listened to her. She was usually right when it came to picking out outfits. "Thank you," I said, laying the outfit on my bed next to her.

"Troy said he couldn't keep his eyes off you and that this Alisha was a bridezilla. He said she was completely rude to him in front of the three of you the entire time, and that it was super awkward. And I guess he winked at you? Is that true?" She practically squealed like a little pig.

"Yes, it's all true, but it doesn't matter. He's getting married, Lil," I reminded her.

"Hey, he's not off the market until he says 'I do'. And it sounds like they aren't going to make it that far anyway," she tried to reason, but I shook my head.

"I'm not going to do anything, Lily. Plus, I probably won't ever see him again, until the wedding anyways. It's all in Mom's hands now. There are more fish in the sea. More available ones too, that aren't already with another fish."

"Yeah, but no one wants to marry a barracuda. That's just asking for trouble," she smirked and left, with me standing there, wishing people weren't so forward in sharing their opinions.

Lily and I finished getting dressed, and she helped me with my hair and my makeup. She decided to go with a wavy-curly-messy side bun and smoky eyes. I was hesitant about the darker eye shadow, but Lily insisted you could always go darker for the evening and get away with it.

Kylee and Susie came over before we left for the party and were surprised to see me dressed and ready to go as well.

"Lily, is your sister *really* going to this party?" I overheard Kylee whisper to Lily.

"Yep, I am Kylee," I responded before Lily could. "I'm going to go to this party. Just don't expect me to stay long. Especially if the food sucks. And if the food sucks, I'm leaving earlier than I've planned to. Where is this place anyways?"

"It's being thrown by someone in your class, but I heard there might be some juniors coming," Susie giggled excitedly.

"How did you guys get invited?" I asked.

"My older sister is a junior and she's letting us in... not to mention that we now have you," Kylee explained and crossed her arms. "Apparently, most of the senior class was invited."

"Well, hopefully I count as most of the senior class. What time is it?" I wondered whether to pull my phone out of my pocket, but Susie beat me to it her phone was in her hand.

"It's time to go. Kylee, do you want to drive?" Susie asked while heading toward the door.

"Yeah, no. I'm driving. I've seen how you clowns drive and there's no way I'm getting in the car with you people unless *I* drive," I informed them and they looked shocked at how forward I was, but I couldn't help it. I'd seen Kylee go over curbs and drive so close to cars, they practically touched. Susie was a texting and driving fool, and Lily never learned to stay in between the lines on the road; she liked to drive right down the middle.

"Fine with me." Kylee shrugged. "It will save me a little bit of gas."

"Where is this party anyways?"

"It's at a house outside of city limits. I've heard it's like a mansion," Susie told me excitedly.

"Hopefully, there will actually be a sitting room." Lily swung her purse over her shoulder. "I'm ready. By the way, we should probably take two cars because Rosie is going to bail super early."

"Oh, that's a good point. Then I'll just follow you guys," I said to Susie and Kylee, and they nodded in agreement.

"Great, let's go!" Kylee opened the door and motioned for everyone to walk out.

The three girls decided to ride in Kylee's car together, which left me alone in mine. Quite frankly I was grateful, because sometimes Susie and Kylee could be too much. Plus, they were probably trying to figure out who was all going to be at this party and texting a bunch of boys. They were boy-crazy. My sister hadn't been a boy-crazy fool, because of the whole Jake situation, but she was slowly getting used to the idea of dating again. She definitely was getting herself out there.

I followed Kylee and I made sure to give her plenty of space, in case she had to slam on the brakes from following the car in front too closely. We first drove through town, where I saw her almost hit a stop sign, a mailbox and a kid crossing the road on his bike. Once we started to slowly exit the city limits, the roads were wider, so it gave her more space to drive. This didn't, however, stop her from running over a flock of quail.

The house didn't take too long to get to and calling the place a "mansion" was an understatement. The house was a three-story Craftsman, pale white with black trim; a huge porch wrapped around the entire house and had another porch on the second level. There was a huge four-car garage off the side of the house and a huge shop in the back. Needless to say, the house looked big enough to house four families.

There were already a lot of cars parked and it looked like they were having someone direct parking off to the side of the house in a field. I did as the attendant directed, and parked alongside Kylee. I jumped out of the car and met the girls behind Kylee's.

"Rosie, do you see how big this house is?" Lily asked, her eyes hungrily regarding the house.

"Oh, that tiny thing? No, I must have missed it driving up the driveway," I said sarcastically and she rolled her eyes at me.

"It's the most beautiful house I have ever seen," Susie said dreamily. "They even have lights lining the driveway and the path, and there are flowers everywhere. Did you notice the fountain in the round driveway?"

"No, I was busy driving and making sure I didn't drive into a ditch, which Kylee narrowly missed, although I did see a few things that she didn't miss. Do you have a bunch of birds on the front of your grill now?" I teased.

Kylee walked to the front and started laughing. "There's one stuck underneath my car. I'll have to see if my dad can get that out later. I'm not touching it."

"I'm surprised there's not more stuck on there. Did you see how fast she was going?" Susie looked at Lily and they both started laughing.

I rolled my eyes and started walking toward the house. "You people scare me. This is why I refuse to ride in that car with you guys. Those poor quail didn't stand a chance."

The three of them laughed again and as we got closer to the house, I noticed the fountain that Susie had mentioned from before. It was gorgeous; it had a path of stone leading up to it for people to walk up to, with lights shining on it, and perfectly trimmed roses of every color surrounding it. It looked like the landscaping had been taken care of on a regular basis, because I didn't notice one weed. The grass had been recently mowed and edged, and bushes also neatly trimmed. It was a gorgeous courtyard, and I was excited to see the rest of the house.

We walked up to the door, where two other girls were standing and giggling about something. Susie knocked on the door. Without hesitation, the door swung open and revealed a maid who pointed us in the direction where music was playing and loud laughter resounded.

We walked down a lengthy hallway, which opened into a fancy den with couches and chairs. There was a huge table filled with every snack and treat imaginable. The back wall was covered by French doors that opened to the rear patio, where most of the party was gathered.

There was a bunch of people from my class that I recognized but had no interest in talking to. I immediately felt uncomfortable and wanted to head over to the snack table. Kylee and Susie found their usual group and rushed over to talk to them. Lily stood by me.

"Are you going to be okay, sis, if I go join my friends?" Lily asked, concerned.

"Yeah, I see chocolate chip cookies over on the dessert table, so I think I'm going to binge-eat." I laughed nervously and smiled encouragingly at her.

"Oh come on Rose, there has to be *someone* here you want to talk too," she said, exasperated, and waved around to the many people giggling and enjoying the party.

"No, Lily, there *really* isn't. I mean, these are people that I am merely acquainted with, I don't actually talk to a lot of people at school and oh my gosh..." I noticed somebody sitting on the couch with a couple other guys.

"What?" Lily gazed frantically around the room, trying to find where my eyes were looking. "What did you see?"

"Nick is here," I whispered, forcing myself to turn away and not stare at him.

"What? Where?"

I peered back over toward the couch to make sure I was really seeing who I thought I was seeing, and then looked away again. "He's the one in the jeans and white V-neck t-shirt. He's sitting and talking with a couple other guys on the couch."

I waited for Lily to find him and heard her gasp. I looked at her and she was smiling like an idiot.

"Rosie. He is *hot*. Like, you know, those hot firemen calendars desperate housewives get? He could be on one of those!"

"Great, now I'm never going to get that image out of my head," I muttered and put my hand on my forehead.

"Is that really a bad image to have?" she giggled and kept staring at him. "Are you going to go talk to him?"

I shook my head. "No way. That would be so awkward. The last time I saw him, he and his fiancé were practically fighting in front of me, Mom and Troy! Speaking of, isn't she supposed to be here?"

"I'm sure she is somewhere. So, what are you going to do? Avoid him all night?" she asked with a furrowed brow, unable to stop staring at him.

"Well, first you're going to stop staring at him and second, yes, I am. Third, I'm going to text Troy and see where he is. Maybe he needs a wingman, or woman," I decided aloud, pulling out my phone and texting him. "You go with your friends." I waved with my phone in their direction. "I'll be fine. I'm in desperate need of a cookie."

"Okay, if you say so. I'll catch up with you in a little bit. Although, I doubt you'll move from the cookies," she winked and I made a face at her.

"Cookies are my safe spot. Go, have fun," I insisted and watched her walk over to a very excited group of freshmen.

I did exactly what I said I was going to do and got myself a cookie. I leaned up against the wall with it and scanned the room. I didn't know over half the people here and had no desire to mingle with anyone. I kept finding myself staring at Nick, who hadn't noticed my appearance, thank heaven. Hopefully, I could stay hidden from him the entire time I was there. If I saw him glance over, I would make sure to put my head down and pretend to look at my phone.

Troy finally texted me back, letting me know he was outside and that he would come find me by the refreshments, and to save him a cookie. After a few minutes, I was on my second cookie and I finally spotted Troy walking in my direction.

"Is that my cookie?" he teased and tried to take it from my hand.

Before he could get a hold of it, I stuffed the rest of it in my mouth and he started busting up, very loudly. This caught some unwanted attention, including Nick. He looked around to search for the familiar laugh and spotted me and Troy. He immediately stood up and started heading in our direction.

"Um, I think you better you swallow the cookie fast" he murmured as he watched Nick walked over.

"I'm trying," I tried to say with my mouth full, but I wasn't able to make out words.

He turned to look at me and started laughing, "I bet you wished you had shared your cookie now!"

I narrowed my eyes and covered my mouth to try and get the blasted thing swallowed.

"He's getting closer."

As if I didn't see him getting closer. I held up my hand to assure him I almost had it down, then decided to turn around to keep some of my dignity. I could feel Troy tap my arm repeatedly, which was his way of telling me to hurry up. Finally, I swallowed the cookie and spun around quickly, and found myself face to face with Nick, praying I didn't have any cookie crumbs stuck between my teeth.

"Hey guys, I didn't know you would be here," Nick greeted us and reached out to shake Troy's hand.

Troy shook it and they smiled at each other. "How are you doing?"

"I'm doing good. Enjoying the party?" Troy asked, smirking at me while I was trying to quickly wipe away leftover cookie crumbs.

"Yes, it seems to be going well so far and no one has tried to show up with any booze, so that's always a relief. Whenever alcohol is involved, fights break out and people act just plain stupid. The last thing I need is one of my mother's art pieces broken again," he rambled on and reality struck me.

"*You* live here?" I asked, shocked.

"Yes, I do. This is my parent's house. My friends wanted to throw a party, and my parents didn't mind as long as there wasn't any recklessness, and I had the biggest home, so the party ended up here," he chuckled and looked around.

"Well, so far so good. I haven't seen any craziness yet, besides a few people trying to choke down cookies," Troy teased and chuckling.

This is where I took it upon myself to hit him in the arm and then smiled at Nick. "Well, your home is beautiful, not to mention it's absolutely gigantic," I complimented him.

"Thank you. You should see it in the spring, when the flowers are blooming; it's my favorite time of year. My mom likes to hold a lot of tea parties in the backyard. In fact, that's where the wedding is being held," he informed us. "Why don't I take you guys back there and show you around?"

I shook my head and tried to play cool. "Oh, we don't want to pull you away from your friends. We can go back there and look ourselves."

"Those guys?" He pointed to the couch where he was previously sitting. "We were just talking about fantasy baseball. The conversation was boring anyways, and two guys were getting way too into it and started arguing about their pitchers. I'm getting whipped again this year, so I have no interest in talking about it."

"I love fantasy baseball! I traded one of my players last night and he ended up getting hurt. I'm so frustrated," Troy said excitedly. I'm sure he didn't expect them to be talking about something they both have in common.

"My pitcher had a terrible game last night and allowed in way too many runs. I'm debating on trading, but there aren't very good options. Maybe you should join our league next year? It's always good to mix it up and bring on some new people to throw off the bracket," Nick offered and pulled out his phone to look at something. "Maybe it will even help me out."

Troy chuckled at his joke. "That would be great, thanks!" Troy looked at me and stuck out his tongue when Nick wasn't looking and I thought about hitting him again, but then Nick looked up.

"This wedding planning is giving me a headache," he muttered, texting back quickly.

"Where is the bride-to-be?" Troy raised an eye brow.

"She's out with her mother tonight, shopping for centerpieces. She had no desire to come to the party," Nick told us.

An awkward tension fell over our conversation and no one dared to comment. It felt too much like a trap. It was weird that she wasn't here for Nick's party.

"Come on, let me show you the back," Nick finally offered, filling in the awkward silence.

I took a deep breath and smiled, trying to appear friendly.

"Okay, great," Troy said and gave me a nudge.

"Awesome," I said simply and followed Nick and Troy out the French doors.

I passed Lily and her group of friends, and she started jumping excitedly up and down. I didn't understand why, because the guy was about to be married. There was no reason to be excited and hoping for anything.

The backyard was absolutely gorgeous and outshone the front of the house. There was an even bigger fountain, surrounded by a garden of flowers and nicely trimmed hedges. There were willow trees with all branches cut to an even length and, in the back, it opened up onto a huge meadow of lush green grass. A pool house and tennis courts were off to the back of the garden and what looked like stables stood off to the right of the property. Basically, the house had everything anyone could ever imagine a rich person having. It sounded like there was an outdoor pool somewhere too, and people were playing in it, but I couldn't see it.

"This place is beautiful," I whispered and Nick chuckled.

"This is like the best backyard ever," Troy said, using the best words he could conceive of, sounding like a thirteen-year old.

"Thank you. My mother takes great pride in her garden and flowers. She has gardeners tend to it daily."

"Well, it definitely pays off. It's gorgeous," I declared.

Nick took us on the path that trailed through the entire garden and Troy started bombarding Nick with questions about his fabulous life. I was watching the people standing around, engrossed in their own private conversations and enjoying time away from the loud music and animated groups inside. Some, however, were taking advantage of the privacy of the garden, and it was awkward.

Nick and Troy were talking about whether he took advantage of the tennis courts often, and I spotted a familiar face stuck on someone else's face. They were sitting on a park-type bench in the back corner of the garden, where no one else was.

"Jake?" I asked, hoping that it wasn't who I thought it was.

Nick and Troy stopped talking, instantly curious.

The couple pulled away from each other and my worst fears were confirmed when Jake and I locked eyes.

"What in the world?" I asked, but was overshadowed by Troy, who was much angrier than I was.

"What are you doing here, Jake? Don't you know Lily is here?" He was, clearly upset.

Nick stayed and I could imagine how confused he probably was.

"Oh, she is? Well, why don't you go ahead and tell her I said hello? Now, if you excuse me, I was busy with Miss Katherine." He chuckled and the girl giggled excitedly.

"Well, this explains everything," I muttered and started to march away, but then Jake stood up and I stopped.

"Explains what? Why your sister is a complete prude and didn't think after four years that I deserved a little something after being her 'precious boyfriend'?"

I spun around very slowly, trying to process what I had just heard come out of Jake's mouth. "Excuse me? What did you just call my sister?"

"A prude. Because that's what she is. She didn't tell you? I set up the most perfect date for her. We spent the day shopping for her, going on a hike, then went to her favorite restaurant, and when I offered a hotel to stay in that night with me, she told me no. Saying that she was trying to protect her precious flower for when she gets married. Because, apparently, four years stuck with her isn't enough for me to finally get anything out of the relationship." His voice had been slowly growing louder with each word and a crowd had started to collect.

"No, she didn't tell me anything, but you know what? Good for her. I'm proud of her, because she was able to stand on her own two feet and tell you no. She must have seen your true colors and realized that you were just a pig," I bellowed and realized that I was starting to shake from anger.

"Oh? Coming from the nun? You Harrison women are all the same. You push away people who actually want to be with you and be close to you. You women are selfish and only think about yourselves," he retorted with a smug look that put me over the edge.

Slowly, I started toward him, unsure what I was doing, but it seemed to please him, because he grew a wicked grin. "So, just because she wouldn't go to that hotel with you, because of a promise she had made to herself years ago, that makes her selfish? And now your looping me and my mom into this? Is that what you're telling me?" I was pretty sure steam was coming out my ears.

"Yes. It makes all of you manipulative, selfish, prudish women who will all die alone, because all you're concerned about is yourselves and your so-called self-worth. Well, you can go ahead and keep your legs crossed. I was bored anyways. I needed someone with a little more ... excitement." He smiled haughtily and put a finger under Katherine's chin.

"Well, if that's how you really feel." I drove my knee into his groin and then punched him right in the nose with all the force I could muster. Upon impact, I felt pain shoot through my hand, but refused to let weakness show as I watched Jake drop to his knees.

He had one hand on his lower region and one hand on his nose, blood oozing between his fingers.

"Good luck getting any excitement now," I said smugly, holding my hand. The adrenaline was wearing off and my hand was throbbing.

"You stupid..." he started to say, but was cut off by Nick.

"I wouldn't say that next word if I was you," Nick advised coolly. "Once you're able to get a hold of yourself, I want you to leave immediately, without making any more problems. Seems like you have more than enough now."

The three of us turned around and found over half the party standing around, watching what happened, including my sister.

"Alright, you guys, break it up, nothing to see here! Go back and enjoy the party," Nick stated and the crowd dispersed. He put an arm around me, which I thought was very forward, and guided me to the house. "Let's go put some ice on that hand. I can imagine it hurts pretty bad."

I nodded. "I'm pretty sure I broke or sprained something."

He chuckled and rubbed my arm, "Well, it was the greatest punch I have ever seen."

"Rose, people are going to be talking about this for months. I've never been so proud! I never thought you would ever do that!" Troy said excitedly.

Lily intercepted us before we walked out of the garden and looked at us sheepishly, "So, I guess now you know."

"Oh, Lil, I'm so sorry. I can't believe what he did to you. I hope you didn't hear too much of that. You deserve way better than that slug," I assured her and smiled. "It's going to be okay."

"I just can't believe you just kneed him and punched him like that. That was probably the greatest thing I have ever seen," Lily exclaimed.

"And well deserved," Nick added. "No woman should ever be talked to like that. It's clear he has no respect for women. I'm going to get in touch with my security and make sure he is escorted off the premises."

"You have security?" Troy started playing twenty questions again as the four of us walked back to the house.

Nick showed us into the kitchen, handed me an ice pack, and invited us to sit in the kitchen for a little quiet. He asked us to wait until he was sure Jake and his "mistress" were gone so Troy, Lily and I sat around the table and waited for him to come back.

"Thank you for what you did," Lily whispered. "I didn't want to tell you what happened, because I was ashamed. I didn't want people to look at me as a prude. Is it so wrong to want to protect something and save it for only one guy? He was so mean to me and reacted terribly when I told him I wasn't going to stay the night with him." She put her head in her hands and started crying.

Troy wrapped his arms around her and let her cry into his chest. "I think it's pretty cool that you're waiting for someone special. Don't let anyone try and convince you otherwise and change your perspective."

I nodded in agreement, "He's just a pig that clearly only cares about one thing. And, sis, you don't have to be afraid to tell me anything. I'll never judge you and you should never be ashamed for standing up for what you believe in." I smiled at her and she smiled back.

"I know. I just can't believe he showed up to the party with her. I mean, what a disrespecting selfish jerk!" She was getting worked up, but Troy quietly shushed her and rubbed her back.

"It's all over now. I think he'll leave you alone, especially if you have Rosie around. No one is going to mess with her!" Troy started laughing and the two of us burst into laughter.

We heard the door open and saw Nick walk in. "Well, he's gone. I'm so sorry about what happened. How's your hand, Rosie?"

"Well, it's numb now, so it doesn't feel too bad." I carefully stretched out my hand and was able to open it completely, without it feeling too bad. I decided I must have merely have bruised it, which was a relief, because I really didn't want to go to urgent care.

"Good, I'm glad. Is there anything else I can do for you? Can I get you a cookie, Rosie?" Nick teased and I chuckled.

"No, I think I'm good. I'm going to go home. I've had enough excitement for one day," I decided and looked at Lily, who still had tears in her eyes.

"Yeah, I think I'm going to go with her. I don't feel like hanging around people anymore. I just want to sit on my own couch and eat an entire bag of chips," Lily admitted and Troy laughed.

I snorted and shook my head. "Figures. Good thing I bought several bags earlier this week."

"Do you want me to drive you home? Neither of you look like you could drive right now," Nick offered and before I could deny the offer, Troy spoke up.

"I'll take them home. I actually came with a couple of my roommates, so I didn't bring my car."

"Thanks, Troy," Lily sniffled and I smiled.

"Yeah, thanks Troy."

The three of us stood up from the table and Nick followed us out to my car. Troy helped Lily in, which I thought was very sweet, and I handed him my keys. Before I climbed into the car, Nick cleared his throat.

"I really am sorry about tonight."

"I am too. I shouldn't have let him get to me. At least, I didn't break something of your mom's," I smiled.

"Just Jake's nose and his manhood," Nick teased.

I giggled and wiped the hair from my forehead. "Yeah, I guess you're..." I watched Nick wipe the stand of hair that persisted in hanging in my face "right."

"Can I get your number, just so I can check up on you and

make sure your hand is alright?" He smiled and waited for my response.

"Oh, sure," I agreed and he entered the digits while I provided my phone number.

"I'll text you right now, so that you have mine too. I guess I'll see you around." He opened the car door and extended his hand for support.

I climbed into my seat and he buckled me in. There was a second when his body was so close to mine, I could hardly breathe. "Thanks Nick, f-for e-everything," I stammered.

"Thank you, for making this night way more entertaining than it ever would have been," he chuckled and smiled at me in a way that took my breath away.

"I second that," Troy laughed and Lily rolled her eyes.

"I'm glad I could be everyone's entertainment tonight," I said sarcastically.

"Me too, I'm glad you came. See you later, Rosie." Nick smiled and closed the door, then Troy started backing out of the parking space, and headed toward our apartment.

Lily spun around in her seat to eye me suspiciously, "What was that all about?" she asked.

"I have no idea." I smiled to myself and looked out the window.

Lily didn't bother asking anymore questions and decided to face forward in her seat. I thought she was a little disappointed with my answer, but it was the honest truth. I had no idea what was going on.

CHAPTER 9

Nick texted me the next morning, while I was still laying in bed, asking how I was doing and how my hand was. I let him know that I was just fine and thanked him for his concern. He replied back with a winky-face emoji, which I had no idea how to interpret it and, so, I decided to not respond and jumped out of bed.

I headed straight for the bathroom to get ready, and was startled to find Lily and Troy asleep on the couch. When we all got home last night, I only talked to the two of them for a minute and then went into my own room to sleep. I figured that Troy was going to head home after dropping us off and making sure we were okay. I definitely didn't expect him to still be on my couch on a Saturday morning.

I walked toward the couch to survey the scene and saw that Lily had her head in Troy's lap, passed out, and Troy was still sitting but his head was leaning up against the back of the couch, his mouth hanging open. It was pretty hilarious and I was tempted to drop something in there to wake him up, but decided not to. We all had quite a night and they deserved to sleep.

I snuck back toward the bathroom and did my usual morning routine, trying to be quiet, and then tiptoed back into my room to throw on some sweats and a t-shirt. I returned to see if either was stirring, but no luck, so I grabbed my laptop and decided to get ahead on some homework at the kitchen counter.

About halfway through an assignment, I heard movement from the couch. I turned and saw Lily slowly sitting up, trying not to wake up Troy, and when she saw me watching her, her eyes grew big. This must have snapped her out of her daze and she stood up quickly.

She walked over, shaking her head in disbelief and leaned on the counter. "We must have fallen asleep talking last night," she whispered.

I snickered quietly, trying not to be too loud. "Apparently. How late were you guys up?"

"I think it was… two?" She didn't sound sure.

"Two in the morning?" I screeched quietly. "We got home at, like, ten last night. What did you guys talk about?"

"Everything. Jake, me, you, him, college, family, you and Nick, the bakery, our future," she rattled off, watching Troy sleep. "We touched on everything."

"I thought he would have left after I went into my room. I had no idea he was going to stay that long. Let alone, spend the night! We've never had a boy stay the night! Mom would kill us if she found out." I put my head in my hands, trying not to think too much about what our mom would say.

"That's why we are not going to tell her. What she doesn't know, won't hurt her. Besides, it's not like we live in her house anymore," Lily tried to reason in an endeavor to make me feel better, but it didn't work.

"Except for that she employs us, and basically helps us pay for our rent," I reminded her and crossed my arms. "It will be fine. It was an accident anyways. It's not like you guys meant to fall asleep, right?" I raised a questioning eyebrow.

"No! No, no, no, that was definitely an accident. I stand by my prudish self, not until I'm married." She used the same vocabulary as Jake; it made me feel bad.

"Lily, you are not a prude. Jake said terrible things last night that were simply not true. He was being completely selfish and, quite frankly, being a boy with only one thing on his mind," I explained. "Remember what Troy said? He thought it was pretty cool, you saving yourself, and I bet many others do too, or they wish they had."

"I know. I just can't believe I used to date that guy. The things he said to you, and how he treated you last night was terrible. I think I dodged a bullet..."

She had wanted to marry the boy so badly just a couple months ago. It was amazing what you found when people's true colors showed through.

"I would say so. Can you imagine being married to that? That would make for a really hard marriage. Everything happens for a reason," I said and smiled.

She gazed downward, looking like she was about to cry, and I patted her arm. "Hey, it's going to be okay. There are more fish in the sea. Besides, I think you can doubt ever seeing Jake at one of Nick's parties ever again."

"I can't believe he had security on hand. Will *you* go to one of his parties again?" she asked, smiling deviously.

I laughed nervously, "No, I probably won't, actually."

"But why?" Realizing how loudly she'd said that, she covered her mouth.

We watched Troy for a minute to make sure he didn't wake up, and then she started talking again. "He obviously liked you being there, and the moment he saw you, he came to you. Why don't you? And he asked for your number. That's got to say something."

"Lily, I feel like I've said this about a dozen times, but he's engaged to another woman. In a few short weeks, he's going to get married and that's that. Besides, he was probably just being friendly. He seems like the type of guy who would go out of his way to make sure someone felt welcomed and included. He was the host for heaven's sake; of course, he came up to greet one of his guests."

I could tell she wasn't buying it. "Alright then. Whatever you say. Give up." She pretended to sound defeated, but I could tell she was over-exaggerating.

"There's nothing to give up! He was never mine to begin with. From the moment I've met him, he's been hers and that's not going to change." I was getting frustrated. I felt like no one was listening to me on the Nick subject and it was completely being blown out of proportion.

"He could be yours though," a voice came from the couch.

I spun around to see Troy stretching his arms and standing up. "Good morning ladies," he smiled and sauntered over to the counter where Lily and I were talking.

"No, he couldn't!" I said, exasperated, and closed my laptop. Clearly, I wasn't going to finish the assignment.

"Good morning, Troy, do y'all want breakfast? I thought about French toast and eggs. I think we have some orange juice too," my sister offered and looked in the fridge. "Yep!" she reached in and pulled out a half gallon of orange juice. "Right here. Anyone want some?"

"I'm game," Troy answered. "What time is it?"

"It's ten. I'll take a little too, Lil, thanks."

"You're welcome," she sang and poured small glasses of juice and then got started on making breakfast.

"Who's working at the bakery this morning?" I asked, panicking a little, wondering if I was supposed to go in this morning.

"Your mom has got it covered, remember?" Troy reminded me and drank the juice. "You put enough time in this week. You work way too much. You were there almost everyday. How do you keep up on all your school-work?"

"She has no social life," Lily called out. "If she's not here, she's either at school or at the bakery. She hardly goes anywhere else well, except for the party last night."

Lily handed me a bowl and some eggs, which meant she wanted me to crack them; she was known to let shells slip through.

"That's because someone was giving me a hard time about having no social life, so I decided to prove you wrong and get out of my very safe and comfortable bubble," I retorted and started cracking eggs.

"Well, I don't think anyone will be giving you a hard time anymore, Rose," Troy chuckled and Lily joined in.

"No, definitely not after last night! Kylee texted me last night and said people had videoed the fight and posted it on social media. No one is going to be messing with you, sis!"

Lily cackled along with Troy and I put my head on the counter.

I felt Troy's hand rub my back, while he was still laughing of course, but still attempted to make me feel better. "Hey, it's all good. Jake got what he deserved. If you hadn't punched him, I was going to. That guy was a rotten piece of work. After that being blasted all over social media, I doubt he will be having any dates anytime soon. How's your hand by the way?"

I turned my head, while it was still on the counter, to look at Troy. "It's a little sore, but not bad. I think I just bruised it." I held it up to see if I could notice any bruising, but I wasn't a doctor, so I had no idea; there wasn't anything noticeable.

"Well, I gotta say, you have quite the right hook. Did you fight in high school?" Troy teased and I rolled my eyes at him.

"No, she was even less social. Don't worry, Rose, we still love you, no matter what. And on a more serious note, thank you for sticking up for me. I don't know what I would have done if I saw him kissing that broad last night. I probably would have had a breakdown."

I sat up and saw that my sister was half-smiling out of embarrassment.

"No one would have blamed you. What he did was a low blow. Who shows up to a party and makes out with another chick? You'd only been broken up for a month and you guys were together for four years! He's a pig," I concluded and she gave me a hug.

"Thanks, sis," she repeated in my ear and we continued to hug. Then I looked at Troy, who was sitting there staring at us and I opened an arm out to him.

"Come in here, big guy. You deserve a hug too," I laughed and he smiled broadly in response.

The three of us had a big group hug and then Lily resumed making breakfast. I didn't know why people gave me such a hard time about not having enough of a social life. In my eyes, I had all I wanted and was perfectly content with it.

CHAPTER 10

Troy stayed for breakfast and we sat around and talked about the events of last night, and then he decided it was probably a good idea to head back to his apartment. He was worried that his roommates were freaking out about where he was, since he'd inadvertently stayed out all night.

Lily and I decided to call our mom and let her know that we weren't going to come home again for the weekend. We felt terrible, but after what happened the night before, we didn't feel like talking about it. But I did make sure to tell her that I made an appearance at the party and hung out with Troy. I also left out the part where I saw Nick, because that would have led to more questions.

Lily went out after Troy left, claiming she was going to study with Susie and Kylee, but I didn't buy it. Knowing those two, they were probably wondering what happened and wanted to know all the juicy details about how I had beat up her ex-boyfriend.

I finished the assignment I had been working on earlier that morning and, once I was done, decided a nice quiet day at home was just what I needed. I didn't want to chance running into people and getting unwanted attention, so I stayed in and watched a movie.

The rest of the weekend, I continued going back and forth between watching movies and studying for upcoming tests. Lily was in and out of the house, not staying around very long, so it was just me. I hadn't heard from Troy since the "sleepover", or Nick.

The following week wasn't very entertaining either. I went to school, turned in assignments, took tests, and worked at the bakery a couple of times. This time, I made sure I wasn't there when Alisha showed up for her meeting with Mom about the wedding cake. However, later in the week, when my mother called to check up on me, she informed me that she loved our desserts so much, Alisha wanted us to cater her bridal shower. She requested sugar cookies with hand-piped buttercream flowers, like the ones that were going to be on her wedding cake. Then she asked if we could provide cinnamon rolls, scones and muffins to a brunch that they were having the morning before the wedding. My mom was so excited, she was practically giggling with excitement. Luckily, everything wasn't for another few weeks, so we had time to plan and prepare appropriately.

However, with the way my weeks were going, the events would be here before I knew it, time was flying by. The closer I was getting to finals, the busier I was. I was studying like a fool, trying to keep up on all my homework, and getting plenty of hours in at the bakery. Not to mention, I was trying to finish everything in order to graduate. The school was nagging seniors to order their caps and gowns. Many students were meeting with their counselors to make sure they had registered to walk this semester, amongst other things.

Lily had completely moved on from Jake, and I believed it. My encounter with him must have been enough to close the book on that chapter in her life. She even saw him hand in hand with some broad walking on campus, and didn't even flinch. In fact, she had been spending time with a different boy lately, but she refused to tell me who. However, this meant she was spending less time working at the bakery, which was really annoying, because that meant I was picking up the hours.

I even had to spend a couple of shifts with Brad. I was mortified when I saw him pick his nose and then get a cupcake for a customer. Fortunately, I intervened before he could touch anything, and made him wash his hands. Twice. Why my mother insisted keeping him on as an employee was beyond me.

She'd been a little quiet on the home front as well. Since I hadn't gone home the previous weekend, I went there to spend some time with her, but she wasn't home. I waited at the house for her to show up, and ended up falling asleep on the couch before I finally saw her walk through the door, which was really disappointing.

The next morning, she woke me up with French toast and eggs, and pretended like nothing happened, which was annoying. All these secrets were driving me crazy and I ended up leaving after breakfast because I was so frustrated.

To be honest, I was feeling like a nobody. My sister was being cryptic, my mom being secretive, and on top of getting ready to graduate, studying and working I, felt like I had no one. I was used to being a lone wolf, but this was too much. I felt plain lonely, and not completely by choice.

The next weekend, I was determined to not be alone. I decided to take my laptop to a popular café on campus and do some studying there. I had no desire to go back to my mother's, because I knew I would have to avoid an awkward conversation, so I stayed home. The weather for May was pretty warm, so sitting outside in a light jacket, and a pair of jeans, people watching, felt really comfortable.

There was lots of foot traffic on this particular street. It had the café, a restaurant, a couple antique shops, a couple clothing boutiques, Mom's bakery, a book store, and even an old movie theater. It was right down the road from campus and a lot of the housing was right behind all the stores, so there were many students who liked to come out and walk along the shops. It was also the perfect place to sit and people watch.

I almost felt pathetic sitting there, watching people for my own entertainment… almost. But, since I didn't have anything else to do, and I was feeling cooped up from being in my apartment, I was desperate. Plus, the sun was warm, and the fresh air was pleasant.

I was sitting at a three-person table and made sure to take up the entire table, so no one thought there was an open invitation to join me. I was sitting in one chair, my feet were on the second, and my backpack occupied the third. I was going through some emails about graduation, when someone caught my eye across the street. It was Nick walking out of Lulu's dress boutique, staring at his phone.

My heart did a little flutter when I saw him, but then it dropped into my stomach when I saw Alisha behind him. I watched them exchange a few words, and then they gave each other a quick kiss before she turned, and walked away. Nick continued to stare at his phone for a minute, and then looked toward the café and saw me staring at him.

I was hoping he didn't recognize me, because I was wearing a baseball cap and my hair was up in a low, messy bun. He started crossing the street and I tugged my hat in a poor attempt to hide my face, and stared at my computer as if to say, "don't talk to me" without actually saying it. Body language was supposed to be an effective way of communication, wasn't it?

While I was trying to pretend to be reading an email, a shadow loomed over me and I found Nick smiling at me. I guess he didn't catch on to what my body language was trying to say.

"Are you hiding from someone? Because I gotta say, sitting out in front of the café in broad daylight on one of the busiest streets is not the best hiding spot," he teased and smiled broadly at me, which naturally made my heart jump into my chest and beat very loudly.

"W-well, I-I,…" I stuttered. I couldn't form words; he had

completely caught me off guard, which was ridiculous, because I had seen him walking in my direction.

I put my feet down from the chair and sat up, thinking it would actually help me form words. "No, I'm not hiding. I was just feeling a little cooped up and since it's been getting warmer, I thought some sunshine would be nice. You know… get some vitamin D."

"Do you mind if I join you?" he asked, still smiling.

"Huh?" I sounded like a caveman. Then I registered what he'd said and gestured for him to sit. "Oh please, go ahead. I don't need three chairs," I said sarcastically, because I actually liked having three chairs. I was quite comfortable, but my view just got a whole lot better, so I let him take one.

Nick laughed and folded his arms on the table. "Yeah, I can tell. So, what are you up to?"

"I've been trying to get through my emails and make sure I'm getting all my things done for graduation," I explained.

"Oh, me too. In fact, I'm sure I have a few emails I should read when I get back home, but I got pulled away to do a little shopping." He sounded a little sour, which I found very intriguing.

"Were you picking out a dress for yourself?" I teased and closed my laptop, realizing I wasn't going to be doing any studying or reading for the moment.

"So, you were looking at me." He pointed his finger at me, chuckling, and my face turned bright red.

"No, well yeah, I guess. I just looked up and you happened to be coming out of Lulu's, so it's not like I was staring or looking for you," I tried to defend myself, but my voice sounded squeaky and pathetic. There was no way he was going to buy my story.

"Sure, sure. I get it. You camp out here and you go looking for guys. Is that what you do every Saturday?" he teased.

"Oh, you bet," I said sarcastically. "I look at every guy and rate them and input my data in the computer."

"What did you rate me at?" he asked and stared, waiting for my answer. He was so handsome and had the most playful expression on his face, it was impossible to look away and not play along.

"A three," I snorted, trying to choke back a giggle. I leaned back in my chair and folded my arms, trying to keep a straight face.

"A three?" he asked, sounding exasperated. "Ouch. Why such a low score?"

"Well, I did see you just walk out of a dress store. That takes you down a couple of notches. And then I saw you kiss Alisha, so technically you're not an eligible guy to collect data on. So, really, you're a zero," I explained, smiling sheepishly, basically admitting that I was in fact staring at him and waited for him to respond.

"Wow, I don't think I've ever been told I was a zero. But it makes sense for your data. I guess you can't rate a guy who is about to get married in a few weeks," he reiterated and eyed me with the cutest half smile I'd ever seen.

I could have sworn that there was a hint of sadness in his voice but I tried not to read too much into it. "How is that all going, by the way?" I asked, wanting to change the subject as quickly as I could. Of course, then I realized I had asked about how his wedding planning was going, and that wasn't going to make the awkward tension go away; in fact, it would make it much worse.

He moved uncomfortably in the chair and answered slowly, "Ah, it's going good. We've got the cake taken care of, as you know, and we were just looking for a flower dress for her niece in Lulu's and ended up finding something, so that's done. We have a meeting with the caterers next week, where I get to taste more delicious food and decide what we want for dinner at the wedding. Of course, whatever we don't pick for the wedding, I'm sure we will end up picking for the rehearsal. She has dress fittings, I have tux fittings, a couple more details to work on and then we're pretty much done." He nodded and we both got quiet for a minute.

"Well," I cleared my throat. "It sounds like everything is pretty much done. My mom was very excited to hear that Alisha wanted her to supply some baked goods for the brunch before the wedding, not to mention the cookies for her bridal shower." I took a deep breath, trying to remember what I wanted to say. "That was nice of you guys to ask her to do that. You've basically made her month and gave her lots of business."

"Well, she really impressed us with her cake tasting, and we knew she meant business. All her flavors were on point. Especially with that thin mint one." He looked up at the sky and sighed dramatically. "I have dreams about that cake."

I laughed louder than I should have and said, "Yeah, that cake never disappoints. Did you guys decide to do a thin mint cake flavor for the wedding cake?"

Nick's face fell a little bit, but quickly recovered. "No, Alisha thought it was a little childish for a wedding and promised to use that flavor for another event."

I nodded slowly, trying to play off the shock, and smiled. "Oh, cool. Well, I'm sure whatever she picked will be delicious and everyone will love it." Well, not everyone, I thought to myself, but didn't dare say it out loud. It wasn't my place. They were clients after all.

"All her cakes were delicious. I have no doubt it will taste and look amazing," he stated.

"She has a gift, that's for sure," I agreed and an awkward silence fell over us again. It was like there was a big elephant in the room, one we both noticed but didn't dare talk about. We both knew the moment we did, it wouldn't be good or appropriate. It was as if there was a silent agreement we had made between us and didn't dare break it.

"Well," I began, "I think I'm going to head to the bakery and get myself a cookie, and say hi to my mom."

The awkward silences were killing me, and I couldn't sit

there any longer. I could only squirm for so long, trying to think of things to say without saying too much. The way he looked at me made me excited and uncomfortable at the same time, which scared me. I knew I shouldn't be feeling any sort of feelings for him... even if he wasn't making it very easy on me and kept showing up where I least expected him.

I stood up and put my laptop in my backpack and gave a little smile. "It was good to see you again," I said politely, hoping he wasn't getting the wrong idea. I hated that I was overthinking every little thing.

"Do you want me to walk with you?" Nick offered and stood up. "I don't have anywhere to be right now, and I could always go for a cookie. Especially your mom's cookies."

I looked at him and felt like I was faced with two options: either tell him no, realizing that he was taken and there was no reason to be entertaining him like this, or take advantage of his offer and spend more time with him.

I never considered myself a selfish person, but I said, "Sure, I'd love the company." There was no harm in walking together and getting a cookie even if I felt like I was doing something morally wrong.

He reached for my backpack, and I pulled back. "What are you doing?"

"I was going to carry your backpack for you," he answered casually. "It looks heavy. Why don't you let me carry it?"

"But why?" I was confused.

"Because, Rosie, I'm trying to be a nice guy and do something nice. Are you going to let me?" he chuckled and held out his hand.

I studied him and tried to decide how I was going to make my decision. He was looking at me, smirking like he knew a joke that I didn't, and continued to hold out his hand. This man was stubborn.

"Alright," I caved, handing over my backpack.

He grinned, took the backpack and slung it over his shoulder, "Geez, what is in this thing?"

"My entire house," I joked and waited for him to get settled.

He waved a hand. "Lead the way."

At first, there was silence as we walked toward the bakery, but then he finally broke it. "So, what are you graduating in?"

"A bachelor in business. What about you?"

"Same thing. I'm going to work with my father after I graduate. Well, technically I work for him now, but I'll be going full-time. He's a successful investor and has been showing me the ropes since I was sixteen. You can imagine how excited he is to see me graduate college and finally move into the working class."

"I bet he's ready to have you there to be his right-hand man."

"I would say so. I think he's been dreaming of this day, ever since they found out I was a boy," he laughed and stopped at an intersection to wait for the light to turn green.

"Are you an only child?" I asked.

"Yes. My mother had trouble conceiving. She calls me her miracle baby," he volunteered nonchalantly and we began walking once the light changed; I followed him, almost speed-walking to keep up with his long strides.

He must have noticed me struggling to keep up, and started laughing, "Do I need to carry you too?"

"Maybe," I shot back. "I'm a short person. I have half the leg length you do."

"I'll carry you if you need me too," he offered again, still laughing.

"Nope, that's fine. I needed a workout today," I said sarcastically and continued power-walking.

"You needed to earn that cookie, right?" he teased and I laughed at the witty response.

"At this rate, I'm going to be able to eat two, no problem," I joked and looked at him.

He was looking at me and smiling with a twinkle in those

beautiful hazel eyes that was unmistakable. Did this guy like me? Or was I just imagining this?

"So, what are you going to do with your business degree?" he asked, changing the subject and making sure to slow down so I could keep up a little better.

"I want to help my mom with her business. Really, I just want to work in the bakery, maybe open up a second one that I can solely run, later on down the road. I really want to bake and decorate delicious treats. That's what I love to do. And to be able to help my mom in any way that I can. She's worked hard taking care of me and my sister, and I want to repay her the favor." I'd became a little somber at the end, and Nick took obvious note.

"Was your mother a single parent?" He seemed a little hesitant in asking the question, but I didn't blame him. It was a hard question to ask, and he probably knew the answer wasn't a happy one.

"Yes. My dad left us when I was eight. It was really hard on my mom, for obvious reasons, but it didn't stop her. She worked full-time, earned a degree, and took care of us girls all on her own. It really was quite amazing. I don't know how she did it all. I can imagine she probably didn't sleep very much, and was tired constantly.

"All along, she was making cakes and other things as a side business, and then it turned into a business, and she opened the bakery when I was in high school. She's turned her dreams into reality, despite the struggles she's been through... she's fought her way out of it. She's my superhero." I smiled amiably, hoping I didn't make him uncomfortable by sharing too much.

He smiled back, and I knew I was okay. "I'd say so. I think she's my new superhero. I can't imagine marrying someone, having kids with them, and then up and leaving. That must have been so hard on all of you," he said softly, his expression sad.

I nodded and tucked my hair behind my ear. "Yeah, it wasn't easy and we didn't understand why he left. I still don't, really.

My mom says that they just fell out of love and he didn't want to live a lie. I haven't seen him since the day he left."

Nick hooked an arm around me and rubbed my arm. "I'm sorry, Rosie, really I am. No one should ever leave their family behind."

I lost my train of thought because a million questions started running through my head. What was he doing? Wasn't he getting married? Was this his way of being friendly? What if someone saw and got the wrong idea?

I decided not to question him, in case I was jumping to conclusions, and let it slide. But I didn't completely understand what he was trying to say through his actions.

Instead, I said, "Unfortunately, we're all human, and are entitled to making our own decisions and he made his. I wish he *hadn't* made that choice, but what can you do?"

We reached the bakery, and he dropped his arm to open the door for me.

"Thanks, Nick." I smiled and walked through the door and found Lily and Troy rather close. I cleared my throat and they looked at me in shock. I didn't know if they were more shocked to be caught, or to see me with Nick.

"Hey, sis," Lily said happily, trying to play it cool, and smoothed out her hair. "What are you doing here?"

"Yeah, I thought you had the day off, Rose," Troy added, copying Lily's casual attitude.

I crossed my arms and walked to the counter, and felt Nick follow close behind me. "Well, I was studying at the café and started craving a cookie. So, I thought I would come by and grab one. I didn't know you two were working together today."

"Mom asked me last minute. She said she had something going on today and needed me to come in, and then Brad said he had some Frisbee golf game to go too. Which, I couldn't believe, if I'm going to be honest, because he's not very coordinated. I can't imagine him throwing a Frisbee very well, if at all," Lily joked, trying to get me to forget what I had just seen, but when she looked at me, she knew I wasn't fooled.

She seemed a little put-out when she realized I wasn't going play off her happy, chipper mood and she crossed her arms and tilted her head; this usually meant she was irritated. "So, were you and Nick studying together?" She gazed back and forth, from him to me and back again, and my face went red.

Nick cleared his throat and answered the question for me. "I saw Rosie sitting outside the café and went up to her to see how she was doing. And then she told me she wanted a cookie, and I thought a little treat sounded good."

Lily slowly nodded and squinted. "A little treat indeed." She nodded again and I just about launched across the counter, but then she spoke again. "So, I guess you guys need a cookie then?"

I rolled my eyes, absolutely fuming, and sensed my nostrils flaring. She had some nerve. I swallowed, and decided a scene wouldn't be the best idea. "Yes, we do. Troy, will you get me the salted-caramel chocolate chip and whatever Nick wants, on the house? Lily, can I talk to you for a minute in the back? I think I left something back there and need your help finding it."

She smiled like she was up to no good. "Sure thing, sis. I would love to help you find whatever you need to find." She turned to walk to the back and I strolled around the counter and followed.

Once I knew we were out of earshot, I gave her a playful push on the shoulder, "Could you be anymore obvious?"

She rolled her eyes in response and scoffed, "Like you were any better!"

"I came up with a great excuse, and you totally ruined it," I complained and she rolled her eyes in response.

"Whatever, it didn't matter. The tension was up the moment you two entered the café." She tried to shift the blame, but I wouldn't let her get away with it.

"Only because we walked in and saw you too hugging or

snuggling, or whatever you were doing!" I pointed my finger at her. "Were you hugging him?"

She nodded, and her smile widened, but she still said nothing, which was very annoying. It was almost as if she enjoyed torturing me. Sometimes, I wished she would just give a straight answer and didn't make me guess what was going on in her crazy life.

"Okay." I started rubbing my temples. "So, was that like a friendly hug or an I-like-you hug? Or we've-been-secretly-dating-and-keeping-it-from-Rosie, because-we-like-to-torture-her, hug?"

Now she was smiling more than I'd ever seen her smile, and was worried her face was going to stay like that. "The last one. And the second one too, I guess."

"I knew it! You do like to torture me," I huffed and sat in a chair.

Lily laughed and sat next to me.

"So you're dating. When did this happen?"

"After he accidentally slept over, we met up and got to talking. Then one thing led to another and we ended up kissing." She started to blush and giggled like a little school girl. "And we've been together ever since."

"Wow, I had no idea. I mean, I did think it was a little weird when you both fell off the radar, and I hardly saw you around the apartment, but I didn't think you guys would be a couple," I admitted and gazed back toward the counter. I could hear Troy and Nick talking.

"Well, speaking of couples, what is Nick doing with you? You guys seem to be running into each other a lot," Lily prodded and raised an eyebrow.

"It's not like we're planning these things. We just... keep bumping into each other."

"You don't think that's weird to you? I mean, it's one thing to bump into each other, but he's choosing to spend time with you. What do you think his fiancé would think? By the sounds of her,

I can't imagine she would be very thrilled," Lily said, her tone serious.

"I know, I know," I moaned. "He put his arm around me and was rubbing it when I told him about Dad leaving us, and it completely caught me off guard! But I didn't know if he was just being friendly... or if it was meant to mean more." I held my head with both hands and closed my eyes. "I don't know what's going on. I don't want to be the *other woman.*"

Lily started laughing and I opened my eyes to see her smiling. "Rose, you are *not* the other woman. But, the way he treated you at the party, and the fact he's choosing to hang around you, is showing a lot. Way more than friends."

"You think? I mean, Troy gives me hugs and wraps an arm around me for friendly comfort. Maybe he's just doing the same thing," I reasoned aloud.

Lily shook her head again. "Nope, he likes you. I'm sure of it and Troy thinks so too." Lily stood up from the table and waved an arm. "C'mon mistress, you must go back to Nick now. We've been back here way too long."

"You are not funny," I mumbled and followed her to the front.

Nick and Troy were still talking and laughing like they were having a good time.

Troy spotted us first and smiled. "Hey guys, guess what? Nick likes going to drive-in movies like we do. So, I thought it would be fun if we all went together, and he said yes!"

My mouth dropped and I gazed back and forth between the two guys. "Oh, did you?" I strained to ask and looked over at Lily, who had a similar expression to mine.

"Troy," Lily began, "don't you think Nick has some wedding planning to do with his fiancé?"

"Actually, Alisha just went out of town for a couple of days, so if that's okay with you guys," he looked at me when he said this "I would love to come with you. I don't have any other plans tonight and, honestly, the last thing I want to do is plan a wedding."

Lily gave me a quick look and smiled at Nick. "We would love for you to come with us. Why don't you two come get us at our apartment tonight, and we'll all go?"

"Sounds great. Do you mind giving me the address?" He was still looking at me, but I was still too stunned to speak.

Luckily, Lily had no problem taking over and answered the questions. "Why don't I get your phone number, and then I'll text you the address? That way you can automatically link it to your GPS." She held out her hand and Nick handed her his phone.

"That would be great," he said cheerily.

There was an awkward silence while Lily entered the number and then texted herself, so that she would have his number. She handed back his phone and he smiled.

"Awesome. Well, I better get going. Apparently, I have emails I need to respond to before tonight," he said, relating back to our previous conversation, which snapped me out of my daze.

"Yep, you probably do. I'll see you out," I offered while walking around the counter.

Nick waited for me and then handed me the cookie I had asked for not moments before. Too bad for me it didn't look appealing anymore. I was queasy now. Regardless of how my stomach was feeling, I smiled warmly and thanked him. Once we stepped outside and we stood in front of the door, I had no idea what to say.

"Did you find what you were looking for?" he asked politely.

For a few seconds, I had no idea what he was asking; then, I remembered my little white lie and shook my head. "Um, no. No I didn't, it must be back at my apartment, I'll have to do some digging when I get home." I felt like Pinocchio and thought my nose would start to grow.

"Bummer, I hope you find it." He smiled encouragingly

I smiled back. "Listen," I hesitated. "You don't have to go

tonight if you don't want to. I don't want you to get into trouble with Alisha or anything." I saw his brow furrow and stopped talking.

"What do you mean?" he asked.

"I just, uh, d-don't, uh," I stammered. I really didn't know how I was going to say this. "I mean, you don't think she'll mind you hanging around me, do you? With Lily and Troy too, obviously. What I'm trying to say is... you don't think she'll be upset if she finds out you've been hanging around me, do you? I don't want to cause any problems... at all." I looked at him, feeling very uncomfortable, wishing I hadn't said anything at all as I waited for him to answer.

"Oh, I see," he nodded and crossed his arms. "Well, I figured we were friends, right?"

His question caught me off guard, so I answered it with a hesitant, "Yes?"

"I think we are too. So, it's not a bad thing for friends to hang around other friends, right?" he asked, smirking.

"No, it's not," I answered flatly.

"Well, that's exactly what I've told Alisha. That I'm going to the movies with some friends, a couple of them happen to be girls, and afterwards we might get some ice cream. I told her the truth and she was fine with it. Does that make you feel better?" he questioned again, his smile more obvious and, this time, I smirked back.

"Yes. I don't mean to be awkward. Like I said, I just don't want to cause any problems between you two. Sorry, I shouldn't have said anything," I apologized and he grinned.

"Believe me, Rosie, any problems that are there, were *not* caused by you," he stated matter-of-factly.

I was a little surprised by how straightforward and honest he was being and, if anything, my suspicions had been confirmed: they *were* having issues.

"Okay," I nodded and tucked a strand of hair behind my ear. It was windy outside and my hair was blowing everywhere. "I won't worry about it," I told him, which was a complete lie, because I was totally worrying about it and was going to continue worrying about it.

"Good. I just want us to have fun together. I think tonight is going to be a blast. I haven't been to a drive-in movie in a while," he admitted and got lost in his thoughts for a moment.

"Yeah, I haven't either. It is going to be fun." I smiled and he smiled back. He had an air of confidence about him, which wasn't arrogant; he knew who he was and he wasn't ashamed of it. I liked that.

"It is. Well, I better get going. I'll pick you up a little later, okay?" he confirmed and I gave a thumbs up.

"I'll be ready," I said, almost sounding sarcastic, and hid it with a smile.

"Great, bye Rosie." He came up to me, gave a hug and walked away.

I immediately walked into the bakery, stunned. I fell into an empty seat, feeling wobbly, and saw that Troy and Lily were staring at me with their mouths open.

"Do you think he knows he's going to get married?" Troy asked, being half funny, half serious.

"Rosie, you have him totally smitten! I think you really are the other woman," Lily squealed and clapped her hands excitedly.

"Lily, why are you clapping? That's not a good thing! Plus, I would never put myself in the position of 'the other woman'." I used air quotes. "Nor, would I ever do that to another woman. That's just not right. Besides, he informed me that he'd let Alisha know that he was going out with a couple of friends and that some were girls, and she didn't care."

"That you know of," Lily mumbled and I gave her the stink eye.

"What am I supposed to do? We keep running into each other and each time I see him, he's really friendly. He's so nice to me and funny, and so handsome. I could stare at that man all day," I said dreamily and Lily looked at me with one eyebrow raised again.

"Are you sure there isn't anything going on?"

I shook my head. "No, sis. There really isn't. Like I said, I wouldn't do that. Dating is hard enough, throwing another woman into the mix would only hurt them. And I don't want to hurt anyone. Maybe I shouldn't go tonight..." I slumped and put my head on the table.

"You can't do that. That would just look bad." Lily said quickly and rushed over to sit next to me.

"Yeah, he's planning on you coming," Troy piped in.

A light bulb flicked on inside my head. "Speaking of, Troy I didn't even say I was going to go to the movies tonight! What was all that about?" I asked tartly. "You didn't ask me if I wanted to go. You just assumed that I would, because he would be there. You're pushing us together and that's not right! He's practically married." I emphasized the last word and huffed, "I literally don't know how many times I have to repeat this, but this isn't appropriate! Someone is going to see us at the wrong place, at the wrong time, and it's going to be bad. I don't want to screw this up. Especially for Mom, who's banking on these orders they made."

"Rose, I just thought it would be fun for the four of us to hang out together, that's all," he defended himself, but I didn't buy it.

Lily and Troy had been excited about the me and Nick, and it needed to end.

I scoffed, "Listen you two, I'll go to this stupid movie. But after this, the Nick-and-Rosie show needs to end. You got it? Don't encourage something that's never going to work out! You're messing with his feelings, never mind mine, and it's not fair!" I stood, feeling myself get upset, and saw Troy and Lily looking guilty.

"Rose, we didn't mean to."

"Yes, Lily, you did. You did, and now I've been put in a very uncomfortable situation. Don't you think this is hard enough for me already?" I croaked, wiping a tear from my eye and then pulling my keys out of my pocket. "I need to go calm down, before this stupid thing tonight. Don't tell Nick anything. I'll do it. But I mean it: no more after this."

I turned around before they could say anything, exited the bakery, and walked home without another look back.

CHOCOLATE CHIP COOKIES

1 cup unsalted butter
1 cup brown sugar
½ cup sugar
2 room temperature eggs
1 tsp. vanilla
1 tsp. baking powder
1 tsp. salt
2 ½ cups all-purpose flour
½ cup semi-sweet chocolate chips
½ cup milk chocolate chips

1. Preheat oven to 350 degrees.
2. Cream together butter, brown sugar and sugar.
3. Add in eggs and vanilla until light and fluffy.
4. Add in baking powder, salt and flour, and blend until just incorporated. Do not over mix.
5. Stir in chocolate chips by hand.
6. Chill dough in refrigerator for about an hour, until cool.
7. Form 1" balls of dough on a sheet tray.
8. Bake for 8-10 minutes. Until edges are golden brown.

CHAPTER 11

I went home and cried.

I cried out of frustration, confusion and hurt. I was trying to be respectful of the situation with Nick and not encourage anything. I didn't understand his personality, if he was being friendly, or if he had feelings for me. I also didn't understand why people seemed to think it was okay to push us together or think it was amusing, like it was some sort of entertainment. They were all enjoying watching the Nick-and-Rosie show, which would most likely be canceled any time now. This couldn't go on. Someone was bound to find out, and the last person I needed to find out was Alisha. I couldn't imagine how she would react if she thought her fiancé had been hanging around another woman.

After I was all cried out, I still had a few hours until the movie and decided to distract myself from my thoughts. I tried to focus on homework but when I realized I had been staring at my computer for minutes on end, I closed the laptop and laid down on the couch. I flipped on a movie that happened to be in the DVD player and tried to watch it, but slowly drifted off to sleep.

The next thing I knew, I heard the door shut loudly, and I was jolted awake. Footsteps neared the couch and I heard a small gasp."Oh, I'm sorry, Rose.... did I wake you?"

I turned my head to look up and gave my sister a sleepy look. "What do you think?" I groaned and wiped my eyes.

"Do you know what time it is?" she asked quickly. "Nick is going to be here in a half an hour! Troy went home really fast to shower and is going to be here soon, too. You need to wake up." She rushed into her room to change. She smelled like frosting.

"I'm not going!" I cried out and covered myself with a blanket.

I heard Lily walk back into the room and marched around the couch. "You're kidding, right? Just because you had a little fit earlier, you think you're getting off the hook?"

"Lily, I just don't feel good about it. What if someone sees us? What if his future wife happens to be going to the movies and sees us together?" I questioned and sat up, so I didn't have to keep craving my neck to look at her.

"It's going to be dark; no one is going to see you. Will you please relax? And stop thinking of it as a date. He just wants to hang out. Him and Troy really hit it off, I guess, and they want to hang out again, and have us there with them. Okay? Like you said, it's just this one time. Pretty soon, he's going to be married and everything will be fine," Lily reasoned with me.

I leaned my head against the back of the couch and sighed. "Fine."

"Thank you," Lily said, exasperated. "Besides, I'm pretty sure Nick wouldn't take no for an answer.... he's really looking forward to tonight." She smirked and walked away.

My sister could be so dramatic.

"You are *not* funny," I called after her.

"Get dressed, Rosie! And put some makeup on. You look like a mess," she called back.

I rolled my eyes and got up to go to the bathroom. I spent the next half hour touching up the puffy bags under my eyes and deciding what to wear. After rummaging through my clothes for ten minutes, I decided on jeans and black zip-up jacket.

Lily came in to check in on me and her face fell slightly. "You're not going to wear a cuter top?" asked the girl wearing a sundress and cardigan.

"You're the one who said it was going to be dark," I sniffed. "Plus, like you said, it's not a date, and I want to be comfortable, especially for a long movie."

"Fine!" She waved her hands in irritation and stomped out of the room.

I heard a knock on the door from my room, and then Troy's laughter. He must have arrived and cracked a joke. A few seconds later, he was standing in my doorway, sizing me up.

"You're going like that?" he chuckled.

I responded by throwing a shoe at him. "You people think you're so funny," I muttered and retrieved my shoe.

"We don't think Rose, we know!" Troy smirked and handed me my shoe. "Are you ready for tonight? Nick just messaged me, letting me know he was on his way."

"Ready as I'll ever be," I said unenthusiastically and walked into the living room.

"Listen, Rose. I'm sorry for making you so upset. I wasn't thinking and should have thought about what I was doing before I opened my big mouth. That wasn't fair of me and I shouldn't have put you in this position," he said, looking guilty.

"It's fine. I'm sorry I reacted the way I did. I shouldn't have freaked on you guys like that. I'm just…" I sighed. "Yeah." I smiled, not wanting to explain further and he put his hand affectionately on my back.

"It's okay. I understand. It's going to be fun, you'll see." He smiled encouragingly, but I wasn't convinced.

"It is going to be fun!" Lily piped up, walking in with fresh makeup and her hair in a cute, messy bun. "You just need to have a good attitude!"

"She kills me," I muttered to Troy and he chuckled.

"What did you say?" she asked, putting her hand on her hip with attitude.

"Nothing you don't already know," I assured her and walked into the kitchen. "Should I pack some snacks? I think we have some bagged popcorn and some candy-"

There was a knock at the door.

"You'd better be ready!" whispered Lily and she pointed her finger at me.

Troy bumped me playfully and smiled.

I rolled my eyes and watched Lily open the door. "Hey Nick, come on in," she greeted cheerfully and I heard Nick say "thank you"as he followed behind Lily.

"Hey, Nick, how are you doing?" Troy walked over and shook his hand, which I thought was very polite of him.

"I'm good. How was work for you guys?" he asked, gazing at Lily and then at Troy.

"It was good," Lily answered nonchalantly. "It went by fast."

"Yeah, it helps when you work with someone you enjoy being around, because then it seems like we're hanging out, having fun, rather than working," Troy added and winked at Lily, who blushed.

I rolled my eyes and started filling a baggy full of M&M's to distract myself.

"How about you, Rosie?" Nick asked stepping across from me, on the other side of the counter. He was wearing white sneakers, a pair of dark denim jeans and a navy colored half zip-up sweater that accentuated his dark blue eyes. His hair was slightly gelled and parted to the side, and all of a sudden, I had this weird desire to comb my fingers through his hair. He looked... absolutely dreamy.

I shook my head in attempt to clear it, and had forgotten what Nick had asked me. "How about what?"

"How was your afternoon?" he repeated with a grin.

"It was good. I finished up my homework and took a nap on

the couch. What about you?" I asked, grabbing popcorn and putting it in another baggy.

"I went home and played basketball with my friend from school. Decided it was best to go through emails, and thank goodness I did. I had a few things I needed to reply to before Monday. Then, I got showered and ready to come here. Pretty laid back, but I think some Saturdays need to be like that." He smiled and I smiled back.

"Yeah, a relaxing Saturday is nice. I definitely needed it after this week..." I noticed that Nick was staring at me, not in a creepy sort of way, but almost affectionately. His eyes were twinkling and I couldn't help but blush. He was so handsome, I was mesmerized; I felt as if I were in a trance. Then I heard someone clear their throat behind me, and I shook myself from my daze.

"Should we get going? The movie is going to start in twenty minutes and we need to find parking spots still." Lily grinned as if she had some amazing secret no one knew but her.

"Well, let's get going then." Nick winked at me before he turned to walk out the door, which made me blush even more.

"Did you get enough snacks there, Rosie?" Troy asked wryly and started chuckling.

"I do. I even packed some for you, but I think I'm going to need all of them now. I didn't eat dinner after all." I squinted playfully and smiled.

"I don't think you're going to eat two entire bags of M&M's," chuckled Troy and put an arm around my shoulders to lead me out the door.

"I'm sorry, but have you met me?" I chortled and Lily started busting up.

"Seriously, Troy, don't you remember staying up late, making cookie dough last year... and you dared her to eat an entire batch, and she finished it?" Lily reminded us between giggles as she locked the door.

"Did you really eat an entire batch?" Nick asked, bewildered.

"Oh my gosh! I forgot you did that. Yeah, she totally did,

Nick. She was so sick afterwards. She kept running back and forth from the bathroom because she thought she was going to throw up!" Troy chuckled and opened the car door, and gestured for Lily to climb into the passenger's seat.

"It was delicious, even though I was up all night with a stomach ache. But I didn't throw up," I said lightly and waited for Troy to open the door for me.

When he started walking around to the driver's side, I stood there confused. Then I looked over at Nick, and he was standing by a brand new Toyota Camry, holding the door. "Oh, I see what she meant by 'spots'," I murmured.

"What?" Nick tilted his ear to hear me better.

"Nothing," I waved it off. "Am I riding with you?" I tried to hide my shock as best as I could, but something told me I couldn't fool this guy. He was very observant.

"If that's okay with you? I assume Troy and Lily are going to be all cutesy and romantic, and you might end up feeling like a third wheel," Nick explained his thought process.

Little did he know, the idea of being their third wheel didn't bother me that much. I *always* felt like the third wheel. When my sister was with Jake, they invited me on some of their dates because they felt bad that I would be home alone. Obviously, this wasn't happening much now, because she had been secretive about dating Troy.

I needed to tell her that hugging and snuggling in the bakery behind the counter for everyone to see *wasn't* very secretive. I had to admit, though, I couldn't decide whether I would rather get a front seat to the Troy-and-Lily show, or spend an entire movie with a guy who was engaged to another woman and about to be married in a few short weeks.

My life was becoming quite complicated. I felt like I was stuck between a rock and a hard place. A few weeks ago, life hadn't proven this hard.

"Yep, that's just fine," I half-smiled and climbed into his car. It had pretty black leather seats and that new car smell. But then

I imagined Alisha sitting in the same spot I was in, and I started feeling a little nauseous.

He climbed into the driver's seat and waited for Troy to lead the way to the drive-in theater, and followed behind.

"Do you know what movie is showing?" he asked, trying to fill the empty silence.

"No, I don't actually. I've heard sometimes they do old black-and-white movies… they're able to get new releases. I think people make requests and vote on them during the week and that's how they decide what to show." I gave my lengthy answer and felt like I talked too much.

"Then I guess it's going to be a surprise." He flashed a smile.

I nodded, and gave a small smile back and he laughed.

"What's on your mind?"

"What do you mean?" I asked quizzically.

"You just seem a little off is all," he pointed out, concern on his face.

"Oh." I tried to think of an excuse fast, so he didn't think I was lying to him. "When I nap, I always feel a little funny afterwards. I woke up not too long ago, so I think I'm still trying to shake it off."

I didn't want him to know that I almost bailed on going to the movies, had a nervous breakdown in front of Troy and Lily, and cried for most of the day…. because of him. Then was caught off guard when I found out that we were going to be alone in a car for the evening. I felt like an emotional rollercoaster.

"Okay, if you say so," he responded and, by the sound of his tone, didn't sound convinced. "I just wanted to make sure you were alright," he said quietly.

I turned to look at him and saw that he was staring at the road with his eyebrows furrowed and his lips pursed. He didn't look angry, or upset, more like confused and lost in his thoughts. It was very sweet for him to be concerned about me. Too bad I was the wrong woman he was supposed to be concerned about, which didn't want me to open up to him at all.

"That's very kind of you, Nick, thank you. I'm okay. I've got my M&M's to perk me up, as long as Troy doesn't challenge me, and popcorn to snack on and wake me up. Nothing like a piece of a kernel stuck in your teeth to keep you awake," I said drolly, trying to lighten the mood.

Luckily, he caught on and chuckled in response. "That drives me crazy. Lucky for you, I keep floss in here, so if you have a kernel bothering you, feel free to grab some."

"Well, look at you. You're like a scout, always prepared. Thank you. I should do that too..." I trailed off, thinking about the only things that I kept in my car: sunglasses, insurance cards, napkins, and a pen. I needed to put more things in it, in case of small emergencies.... like popcorn teeth.

"You're welcome," he chuckled again and pulled into the drive-in parking lot.

It was behind one of the school buildings on campus, with a big white screen hanging from it. There was a little pop-up concession stand where they had overpriced candy and popcorn to sell to poor college students, except Nick. When we pulled in, there were already a few lines of cars parked, so we ended up toward the back, parked by Troy and Lily.

Lily rolled down her window and looked around. "The movie tonight is *Breakfast at Tiffany's*." She sounded excited; behind her, Troy rolled his eyes.

"Oh, sweet! I love that movie. I think Troy does too," I teased and watched him bang his head on the steering wheel, accidentally making the car horn go off.

We all laughed and I started breaking out snacks.

"Hand it over, Rose! Or I'll come over there, sit on you, and take them all," Troy teased, pointing a finger at me.

I looked at Nick and shook my head, giggling. "See? I knew it wouldn't last long. That boy loved his snacks. He can't go through a shift without eating a couple of cookies. Here." I handed a bag of candy and popcorn over to Nick. "Can you please hand these over to Lily, before I have Troy attack me?"

He chuckled and took the bags. "Sure. I don't need a crazy man in my car." He handed the treats to Lily, who shook her head and rolled her eyes.

"This boy never stops eating," she complained and tossed them onto Troy's lap.

"That's all you're getting tonight. There's no coming for seconds over here," I called over and laughed.

"We'll see about that," he smirked.

Lily gave us one more eye roll and then shut her window. I liked it when they had it down, because then we could talk to them and it didn't feel so exclusive. Being in a dark car with a boy caused the sort of tension that was almost too uncomfortable to bear. I gazed around the parking lot to distract myself.

"I don't think I've ever seen *Breakfast at Tiffany's*," Nick admitted. "What's it about?"

"Basically, it's a romance. About a woman who is obsessed with Tiffany's and money, and likes to have her freedom. She's slow to realize that she loves a man, who desperately loves her too, and ultimately decides if money or love is worth it," I explained and Nick became very quiet. "Are you okay?" Had I said the wrong thing to him, or upset him?

"I just didn't realize I would be watching a movie that relates so much to me," he muttered and placed a hand on his forehead.

"What do you mean?" I whispered, debating whether I should have even asked that question.

Before he could answer, the screen lit up and the movie began playing. I pulled out my bag of popcorn and shoved a handful in my mouth. When a couple escaped, I quickly picked up the popcorn from the seat, not wanting to dirty this nice man's car. When I glanced at him to see if he had caught me, he smiled and chuckled. I handed over the popcorn bag and smiled sheepishly, making him laugh even more.

We watched the first couple of scenes, and the furrows on Nick's brow became deeper and deeper.

"That woman is crazy," he would mutter under his breath.

I occasionally looked at him to view his facial expressions during certain scenes. Seeing him looking confused made the movie more entertaining... until he muttered again under his breath. I would stifle a laugh, or try to cover it up with a cough.

The movie stopped about halfway through for intermission and people got out of the cars to head to the snack stand and restrooms. I noticed my own snack bags and couldn't believe that I had eaten all my candy and that Nick had taken out his frustrations on my popcorn.

"I think I'm going to get up and walk for a minute. Do you want to come?" he offered as he opened his door.

"I think I'm going to go see how Lily and Troy are doing. Thank you, though." I started to open my door, but he stopped me.

"Oh, hang on!" He jumped out of the car and jogged around to my side and opened the door.

I smiled, blushed, and climbed out. "Thank you. You didn't have to do that," I stated, smiling from ear to ear.

"Yes I did. You shouldn't ever have to open your car door," he said and shut the door. "I'll see you in a minute."

I nodded and watched him walk toward the restrooms. When he was about a hundred feet away, I walked to Troy's car and knocked on the window.

Lily opened the car door and stood.

"How are you guys liking the movie?" she asked immediately and leaned up against the car.

"I think I'm enjoying it a little more than Nick. He keeps muttering things under his breath, and it's cracking me up. What about you guys? Are you even paying attention to the movie?" I inquired and heard Troy snort.

"Yes, we'e been watching. And Troy wouldn't share any of his snacks.They were gone within the first five minutes!"

I heard Troy bust up laughing in the car.

"She told me she didn't want any!" Troy said loudly enough so I could hear and Lily rolled her eyes in response.

"Troy, don't you know that generally means the opposite?" I hinted and started laughing at him.

"What do you mean?" he asked as he climbed out.

I laughed. "When a girl says that she doesn't want anything, it actually means she does," I educated him and shook my head. "I can't believe you ate everything. Poor Lily!"

"But she said she didn't want any!" He extended his hands in a what-else-can-I-say gesture, and I started laughing even more.

"Women lie, Troy," I exclaimed.

Lily and I busted up, staring at his bewildered face; it was funny, and totally cute.

"Women," he muttered.

I gasped, pretending to be offended, and pointed a finger at him."Hey! You wouldn't have us any other way!"

This time he laughed and extended his hands in surrender. "You're right. I love you, ladies. So, does this mean that I need to go get snacks?"

"By George, I think he's got it!" I teased with an English accent.

"Okay, I'll be back."

"There's no need for that," a voice called out as Troy opened the door.

I saw Nick walking toward us with two bags of popcorn, a couple boxes of candy, and four drinks.

"It must be Christmas!" Lily giggled and Troy rolled his eyes.

"Way to be the hero, Nick," Troy said sarcastically.

Laughing, Nick answered.

"Well, I felt bad eating all of Rosie's popcorn and noticed she had eaten all of her candy, and we have another hour to go on the movie," Nick explained as he handed Lily the popcorn.

Troy eyed it hungrily, but Lily shook her head.

"No way, man, you can have this *after* I'm done." She

returned to her seat and started devouring it; clearly, she was hungry.

We all laughed and Nick handed Troy candy. "I didn't know which soda you liked best, so I got one of each: Dr. Pepper, Coke, Pepsi, and root beer." He waited for us to answer.

"I'll take the Pepsi," Lily said from the car, so I handed it to her.

"I definitely want the root beer. Lily said I shouldn't have caffeine so close to bed. Last time I chugged a Pepsi at the movies, I was up most of the night," Troy admitted and thanked Nick as he took it from him.

"That leaves Dr. Pepper and Coke," Nick said.

"Well, I definitely want Dr. Pepper. It's my favorite." I smiled and took the drink from him. "Thank you. You didn't need to do this."

"I wanted to. Plus, that popcorn made me thirsty, and I figured everyone else would be too," he added. "Should we head back in the car? I think the movie is going to start back up soon."

"You're really into it, aren't you?" I asked teasingly, "And here, let me take that popcorn from you, so you're not carrying everything."

He walked around and opened the car door for me.

"Thank you." He smiled and returned to his seat. "Well, I need to figure why she's so obsessed with this cat. And, whether or not she's going to end up with the nice writer guy. I mean, I'm sure it ends up all happy in the end, but the main character is killing me."

I giggled. "Nick, are you a romantic?"

Nick laughed."No. At least, I didn't think so. But this doesn't really count as a romance movie, does it?"

"Well, seeing how you just said you wanted to know if the main character ended up with the guy, then yes. I would say you're a little bit of a romantic. Not to mention, you are getting married, so you *have* to be a little romantic." I grew quiet after mentioning him getting married and an awkward silence filled the car.

"Well, being romantic is not a bad thing, is it?" he asked sheepishly.

"Nope, not at all," I said confidently and smiled.

"Cool." He smiled in return and the movie started up again.

He was definitely the kind of guy who didn't like to talk during movies. Admittedly, this was tough for me, because I was one that had no problem having a conversation during a film. On the other hand, I had seen this movie a few times already and he never had, so he was probably trying to understand it; it had been a little confusing for me the first time I'd watched it as well.

I sipped my soda and munched my popcorn as I sat there entertained by not only the movie, but by Nick's reactions. With every scene that passed, I would glance at Nick to see what he thought by reading his facial expressions. It was hilarious.

At one point, he caught me staring at him and started laughing "What are you looking at?"

"Nothing." I felt my face flush. Again, I was grateful that it was dark outside and he couldn't see my face turn as red as a tomato.

"You were watching me to see my reactions, weren't you!" he asked and I could feel my face flush even more.

"Maybe…" I wasn't sure how to answer his question. He had caught me staring at him, which was super embarrassing.

He chuckled. "You're ridiculous. And you're eating all the popcorn!" He took the bucket of popcorn away from me and tossed a couple in his mouth, before he smiled and laughed. "I'm only kidding. Here." He handed it back and I took it, giggling.

"I'm just trying to get as much as I can before you start and finish the bucket. I saw what happened with my popcorn baggy," I joked, took a huge handful of popcorn and shoved it in my mouth.

"Well, then I guess I can't blame you," he chuckled and turned his attention back to the movie.

I was hoping he didn't miss a good chunk of the movie from our banter. I began to watch again, knowing there wasn't a whole lot left and that I should let him watch it. I had to try not to stare at him again. Honestly, though, I couldn't help it. His facial expressions were hilarious, and he wasn't bad to look at either.

As I was watching, I continuously reached into the bucket to grab handfuls of popcorn. I realized I was really hungry, which made sense, because I had slept through dinner, and the salty, buttery popcorn was irresistible, way more appealing than the bagged popcorn I had brought from the apartment. While I was going in for another handful, my hand felt his touch the back of mine. This made me jump out of my skin and I instantly withdrew my hand.

"Oh! I'm sorry, I didn't mean to. Go ahead," I insisted and put my hands in my lap.

He chuckled."It's okay, Rosie."

When he said that, it sounded as if he were implying that in relation to something else. This made me wonder what he had meant and I was tempted to ask, but I reminded myself of my promise to *not* bother him anymore during the movie. The last parts of movies were always the best anyways, and I didn't want him to miss out.

I waited as long as I could to get popcorn and when I was sure he had just gotten his own handful, I grabbed some. Relief washed over me as I continued eating handful after handful of popcorn and re-engrossed myself in the movie. I felt like a robot, moving my hand slowly in and out of the popcorn bucket and into my mouth.

I had lost track on when Nick had gotten his own; I reached in the bowl, promising myself that it would be my last handful, knowing I was going to suffer tomorrow with a bloated stomach. This time, I touched the top of Nick's hand. I felt like an idiot, and tried to pull back quickly once again, but this time Nick grabbed my hand and intwined his fingers in mine.

He looked at me and smiled, and then turned his head back toward the movie screen. I sat there, stunned- too stunned to move, too stunned to speak, too stunned to realize what was happening. My stomach started turning into knots, and I could hear my heart beating in my ears, and my body temperature getting warmer.

I was worried that my hand was going to start sweating, so I tried to steady my breathing and calm my body. I really wanted to start panicking and ask him what in the world he was doing, but something in my brain prevented me from doing so. Deep down, I knew I liked him and was incredibly attracted to him, but this was wrong.

I was really wishing I could read minds, so I could figure out what was going on in that head of his. But, out of my own selfish reasons, I didn't dare speak. I forced myself to watch the movie, even though I wasn't paying attention to it... and let our hands remain intwined in the popcorn bucket.

CHAPTER 12

The movie ended and I thought Nick would let go of my hand, but he didn't. It was ten o'clock and I was feeling really sleepy, and didn't feel like fighting him. Not to mention, my stomach was starting to hurt from all the popcorn. Butter and salt were not a good thing to eat so late at night. Especially without water to help flush the sodium. And the soda didn't help my situation at all.

He rolled down the window, the same time Lily did, "What did you guys think?" he asked.

"Boring," Troy called and Lily rolled her eyes.

"Troy just doesn't appreciate a classic when he sees one," Lily teased and Troy poked her side playfully, which made Lily laugh. "What did you think of it, Nick?"

"I thought it was good. Definitely more of a chick flick, but it wasn't too bad. I did like it."

"Good, I'm glad. I think Troy and I are going to grab some ice cream. Do you guys want to join us?"

I groaned quietly, feeling myself turning more and more into a pumpkin by the second, and Nick looked over at me and grinned. "You know, I think we're going to pass this time. I think Rosie is feeling pretty tired, so I'm just going to take her home."

"Tired? Are you serious, Rosie? You napped all afternoon and you're still this tired?" Lily questioned, sounding irritated, but I didn't care.

"You know napping makes me more tired! Plus, I think I ate too much popcorn," I moaned and put my free hand on my forehead.

"Are you okay?" asked Nick, quietly enough so only I could hear.

"Yeah, I think I just need to go lay down," I admitted and leaned my head against the seat and closed my eyes.

"Oh, I bet your stomach hurts big time," Lily called out.

Thanks, Lily.

"Amateur," Troy teased, but I didn't respond.

I was feeling worse by the minute.

Nick was regarding me intently, and I thought he could tell by my face that I truly didn't feel so good.

"Alright, well I'll see you guys later. Thanks for the invite." Nick waved and started to roll up his window, but then heard Lily speak.

"You're welcome. We'll have to do this again!" she said, which snapped me out of my pain enough to give me strength and lean forward and glare at her behind Nick's back.

She noticed, but quickly looked away. "Bye, Nick. See you at home, Rosie. I'll be back by midnight."

I gave her a thumbs up, which was a little awkward since Nick had my left hand and I had to reach over for her to see it. I watched them pull out of the parking stall and Nick followed behind, still holding my hand. I was still too shocked to speak as he drove down the road, back in the direction of my apartment. When he started brushing my hand with his thumb, that's when I snapped. "Nick, what are you doing?"

"What do you mean?" he asked innocently.

I huffed, and lifted our interlaced hands to show what I meant.

"Oh, I see."

"I mean, what is going on? Aren't you getting married? I'm pretty sure this is out of bounds in the friend zone," I bellowed, which was a little loud in the car and I felt bad, but I had to stand my ground- or rather, sit in my seat confidently. Then I clenched my stomach and felt like I was going to be sick.

"Whoa. Rosie, are you okay?" Nick tightened his hold on my hand.

I couldn't tell if I was more annoyed by this gesture of affection, or thought it was sweet.

"I feel like I'm going to be sick," I admitted and put my purse in my lap, just in case I really needed it, then leaned my head against the back of the headrest. "I ate way too much popcorn."

"Okay, well hang in there, we're almost to your apartment," he said consolingly, but my stomach wasn't taking it.

"Okay," I whimpered, and forced back the tears that wanted to stream down my face.

Within a few minutes, we pulled up in front of my apartment complex. As soon as Nick parked, he hopped out of the car, jogged around to my side, and opened the door.

"How are you doing?" he asked.

"I can't decide if I want to lie down or put my face in the toilet bowl," I moaned, and resisted the urge to gag.

Nick chuckled and bent down. "Well, I'll be interested to see how that goes. Come on." He wrapped one arm around my shoulders and tucked his other arm under my knees and pulled me out- he lifted me out of the car so easily, as if I was a feather.

"Whoa! W-what are you d-doing?" I stammered.

"I would hate to see you try and walk, so I'm going to carry you." He grinned and carried me like it was no big deal.

I groaned. "Okay, well don't rock too much; otherwise, things are really going to start moving."

Nick chuckled again, "I'll do my best. Where are your keys?"

"Let me get them." I reached into my purse and pulled out my key-ring that was way too full. It had: my house key, mail key, my mom's key, my mom's spare mail key, the bakery key, my car key, my mom's spare car key, Lily's spare car key, and a couple mystery keys that I hadn't figured out. I wasn't willing to throw them away quite yet, because every time I threw something away, I always ended up needing it. Lily liked to tell me I was going to become a hoarder.

"Here," I held out my keys and realized he couldn't grab them right then. He was carrying me; apparently, my mind wasn't all there. "Oh, never mind. Sorry," I giggled, feeling stupid.

"You're okay," he said. "We're almost there anyway." He sounded tired, which I felt a little guilty about, but I knew there was a slim chance of him putting me down.

I smiled at him and leaned my head on his shoulder, feeling a wave of nausea come and closing my eyes to fight the temptation to vomit. When the wave of sickness calmed, I whispered, "Thank you for carrying me."

"You're welcome, Rose," he said tenderly and carried me all the way to my front door. "Alright, do you think you can get those keys and put the right one in the door lock?"

"Yeah, I think so." I fumbled with the keys as, he brought me close to the door.

I put the key in and unlocked the door.

He walked into my apartment and stood in the doorway. "Okay, where do you want to go? Have a lay down? Or visit toilet bowl?" He chuckled quietly.

"I think I want to lay down," I decided and tried to get down, but Nick held strong. "You can let me down now."

"It's okay, I'll lay you down," he offered and I thought he was going to walk me to the couch, but then he walked into the direction of the bedrooms, which made me uncomfortable. "Which bedroom is yours?"

"The one to the right." I pointed weakly and thanked my lucky stars that I'd cleaned my room recently. I had even made the bed that morning.

He laid me gently on my bed and sat on the edge of the bed.

He looked a little tired and was breathing a little heavier than usual. "I think I got my workout in for the day," he teased, straightening his back to stretch.

"Do you need water? The cupboard next to the refrigerator has cups if you need anything. Or whatever you find in the fridge is good too," I offered and he nodded.

"That actually sounds like a good idea. I'll be right back. Do you want anything?" He asked.

"Water sounds good, thank you," I smiled.

"Okay."

I watched him walk from the room. While he was gone, I quickly took off my shoes, and my jacket, and threw a blanket loosely over myself. I pulled out my phone to see if Lily had messaged me, but there were no messages. She was probably enjoying some time with Troy all to herself. I scrolled through my phone, waiting for Nick to return, still fighting the massive nausea I was feeling.

I still couldn't wrap my brain around what was going on. Nick and I had gone on a "sort-of" date, I got sick, and he carried me to my bedroom, and now we were both in my apartment, *alone*. I was convinced there was no way that Alisha would be okay with this.

Nick walked back in with a cup of water and handed it to me.

"Thank you." I took a small sip. I was nervous I was going to upset my stomach even more, so I decided to take it easy on the water.

"You're welcome. How are you feeling?"

"I'm doing a little better now that I'm lying down. Thank you for taking care of me. I didn't mean to put a damper on everyone's evening," I said, feeling guilty.

Nick chuckled and sat down on the edge of the bed. "You didn't. Buttery, salty popcorn can hurt anyone's stomach. Especially with the amount you ate."

"Hey!" I laughed, pretending to be offended by his joking, "I was hungry. Plus, you ate a lot too, so why doesn't your stomach hurt?" I leaned back against my headboard and put my hands on my stomach; it was starting to cramp.

"It's called an iron stomach," he chuckled. "Are you sure you're okay?" He looked concerned as he eyed my hands.

"It will pass, hopefully. I'll be okay. It's not like I haven't been sick before," I said firmly, attempting to convince him, and shrugged. "I bet I'll feel better tomorrow."

"Alright." He smiled and took a deep breath. "Well, I better be going... it's getting late. Do you need anything before I leave?" He stood and waited for my answer.

"Actually, yes. My iPad is in my backpack by the couch. Do you mind grabbing it for me, please?" I felt a little guilty that I just asked him to do something else.

"Sure, I can do that, hang on. He sauntered from the room and returned a moment later. "Here you are, miss, you're iPad." He handed it over.

"Thanks. I'm thinking I need to watch a movie to help wind down and distract from this achy stomach," I told him, though I had no idea why.

"Cool. What movie are you going to watch?" he asked, as if I had piqued his interest. "Another Audrey Hepburn movie?"

I laughed, "No, I was thinking *Sherlock Holmes.* It's a quiet movie, where I really have to concentrate, and listen to the words and deductions. It usually helps me go to sleep if I'm having trouble drifting off, so I'm hoping it does the trick tonight."

"Well, I hope it works. I don't think I've ever seen *Sherlock Holmes,*" he admitted.

"Wait, what? You've *never* seen Sherlock Holmes? He's the best detective ever imagined, and *Robert Downey Jr.* depicts him perfectly," I exclaimed, all hyper, but I couldn't help it. I was a huge fan of mysteries.

"Wow, I've never seen you so excited about something," he

chuckled. "I've heard about it, but I've never gotten around to watching it."

"Well, then one of these days you're going to have to watch it and let me know if you like it," I said matter-of-factly.

"Well…"

"What?" I drawled.

"How about *now*?" Nick asked cautiously.

"What?" I whispered, feeling my brow furrow.

"Can I watch it with you now?" Nick repeated, clearly looking like he was regretting his decision to ask.

"Are you sure that's a good idea?" I asked warily.

"We've already watched one movie. I doubt a second one is going to make much difference. Besides, I want to make sure that you're going to be okay," he explained, wringing his fingers nervously.

"If you say so," I shrugged. "Let's go watch it in the living room." I started to get up, but he shook his head. "What?" I asked, perplexed.

"Let me carry you out there," he offered.

"N-no, no, n-no," I stuttered.

He ignored me and scooped me up, walked us out of the room, and laid me gingerly on the couch.

I was very aware of his muscular biceps against my body and tried to keep my thoughts in check. "Maybe I should keep you around. I would have my own personal taxi," I teased as I pulled a blanket over me.

"I'll be here as long as you want me here." He sat on the other side of the couch and smiled.

"Sh-should we start the m-movie?" I stammered, not knowing how to respond to his comment.

"Sure, do you have all the remotes you need?"

"Yep, I keep them right here." I reached up. "On top of the couch." I turned on the television and stared at Nick. "I'm curious to see if you're going to like this movie. I might be offended if you don't; it's one of my favorites."

"Well, I don't see you as someone with bad taste in movies, so I'm sure I'll like it," he assured me and watched me get the movie ready.

I was about press play when I glanced over. He was sitting calmly, waiting for me to start the movie, looking very content. I desperately wanted to know what was going on in his brain, but at the same time, I was worried what I might find out if I asked him. Here we were in my apartment, alone, about to watch a movie on the couch in the dark.

Had I mentioned he was engaged because that glaring piece of information was something I couldn't let go. Despite me freaking out on the inside, I couldn't help but feel a sense of calmness as I watched him. He honestly looked happy, and relaxed… not to mention he was so handsome. He was, as my mom would say, "easy on the eyes".

I took a deep breath and pointed the remote at the TV. "Are you ready?" I asked and gave him a half smile.

"I'm ready when you are," Nick beamed and nodded and I had to remember to breathe.

"Great," I whispered and gave him another half-smile. I pushed play on the movie and we waited for it to begin, sitting in silence, both of us clearly unsure what to say.

After a few moments of watching the opening credits begin, he decided to break the awkward quiet. "How are you feeling?"

"A little better. My stomach is still aching pretty good, but I don't feel like I need to hang my head over the toilet anymore," I answered and held a hand over my stomach when it started to ache a little more.

"I'm glad you're feeling a little better. I thought I was going to have to rush you right into the bathroom. I was preparing myself to hold your hair and everything." He started chuckling. "I'm glad it didn't come to that. Not just because I didn't want to hold your hair, I would have, but I'm really happy you're feeling better," Nick restated and smiled again in a way that made my heart skip a beat and my stomach hurt even more.

Wasn't there someone who'd said love wasn't for the faint of heart? "That's very sweet of you. I'm glad it didn't come to that either." I was cut off by the beginning of the movie. "Oh look, it's starting," I pointed out and stopped talking so that he could watch it in peace.

It wasn't the kind of movie where you could talk the entire time and guess what was going on. There was a lot of talking and speculating, and it required all the attention a person could give in order to understand it.

I decided he was way better-looking than *Sherlock Holmes.* I tried to watch the movie… I really did. I couldn't help going back and forth between watching it and eyeing Nick, just like I did when we were watching *Breakfast at Tiffany's.* I don't know why, but I thought he was so entertaining; his face was very expressive. Even if he didn't talk, he could speak volumes through his facial expressions. He was like an open book.

I didn't know when it happened, and I certainly didn't mean for it to happen, but between watching the movie and him, I fell asleep. I must have drifted off without noticing… and then I was out. I was a really hard, deep sleeper; there wasn't anything that could wake me up. And given I fell asleep on the couch regularly, my body was quite used to sleeping on it.

I woke up the next morning dazed and confused. I was squinting due to the bright sunshine shining through the window. I looked around the room once my eyes were able to focus and realized I was on the couch. Then I thought my eyes were playing tricks on me, because on the other end, it appeared as if someone else were fast asleep.

A first, I thought it was my legs, but then I realized it was another body. Sometimes Lily liked to sit on the couch and watch something before she went to sleep, so I figured it was just her. But then I looked more closely at the sleeping body, and realized the body was bigger than Lily's. I couldn't see the face from where I was laying, so I willed myself to sit up and saw that it was Nick.

I covered my mouth to remind myself to be quiet and not wake him up. I saw his legs underneath the same blanket I had been using. I moved my feet and realized my legs were between his. This was so bad.

I wanted to get up, but since we were sharing a blanket and our legs were intwined, I didn't want my movements to disturb him. I was stuck, but I knew I needed to get out of this position, and pronto. I had no idea what to do, and I felt like my brain couldn't properly process anything... because a boy had stayed over at the apartment, again!

I looked around for my phone; I knew I had brought it to the couch when Nick carried me. I peered under the blanket, in the creases of the couch, and underneath me, but I couldn't find it. I looked past the couch and saw it lying on the floor. Slowly, I reached over, trying to keep movements to a minimum, and was able to reach it with my fingertips.

I flipped on the screen and saw there was a message from Lily. It read: "You have a lot of explaining to do." She had sent the text after midnight. She must have had a late night with Troy.

I texted her back, letting her know I was awake. The time said it was just after eight. I didn't expect Lily to wake up anytime soon because, on Sundays, she liked to sleep in as long as she could. I settled back into the couch and closed my eyes, even though I didn't feel at all sleepy, butI didn't know what else to do.

A door opened and my head shot straight up, and I saw Lily emerge from her room. She had a smirk on her face and giggled, shaking her head. I could tell she thought of me as a big hypocrite and was reveling in the moment.

She walked to the couch and looked at Nick, who was still sleeping. She lifted an eyebrow and gestured Nick with her chin. I looked at our sleeping guest and then looked back at her, and felt my forehead scrunch in confusion.

She moved closer and bent over, next to my ear. "By the looks of it last night, things must have gone well," she said smugly and giggled quietly.

I swatted at her, but she had already moved out of the way. She gave another smile and returned to her room.

I laid there, thinking of what she had said and stewed. If things weren't confusing before, they sure were now. I kept wondering what Nick had been thinking, and was tempted to ask, but didn't dare. I wanted to know where Alisha was and where they were in their relationship. After all, they were getting married, so why was he in *my* apartment, sleeping on *my* couch?

I didn't want to ruin Alisha and Nick's happiness. Before I even came into the picture, they were happy and set on getting married. I didn't know about their relationship or their path to get to where they were presently, but I didn't want to get in the way. They didn't deserve that, and I would feel guilty for doing so for the rest of my life. Nick and my relationship, whatever it was, needed set boundaries.

There was no way I could see Alisha being okay with Nick hanging around another girl all night. That just screamed trouble. Things needed to be said, and as much I didn't want to, I had to set things straight.

I slowly pulled my legs from between his, stood up, and quietly went to the bathroom and brushed my teeth. I even used my sister's mouthwash for extra added freshness, because I could tell I had some serious morning breath. I brushed through my messy blonde hair, pulled it up in a high ponytail, and wiped away the smudged makeup under my eyes. I didn't want to look like a complete hot mess when Nick woke up, regardless of how frustrated I felt with him.

Quietly, I left the bathroom and found Nick sitting up, combing through his hair with his fingers.

I walked over and made eye contact. His eyes still looked a little sleep-dazed, but he greeted me with a smile regardless and chuckled. "Well, I didn't expect that to happen last night," he whispered.

"Yeah, that was about the last thing I expected to happen," I agreed and sat on the opposite end of the couch.

"How are you feeling this morning?" he inquired and rubbed his eyes.

"I'm feeling much better. My stomach doesn't hurt anymore, so that's good." I started twirling my thumbs out of nervousness.

"I'm glad you're feeling better. I'm sorry, I didn't mean to fall asleep. I really got into the movie and didn't want to stop watching it after you fell asleep but, as it got towards the end, I think I passed out." Nick turned toward me, so that he was looking directly at me. "I honestly didn't mean to. I should have left sooner… while I was feeling sleepy."

"It's okay. It was an honest mistake. Troy did the same thing a few weeks ago, actually," I informed him, although I didn't know why. I tended to share more information than necessary when I was nervous.

"Huh… that's ironic," he answered honestly and stretched his arms.

"Nick," I said slowly and took a deep breath, trying to find the courage to say what I felt I needed to say.

"Ye-es, Rosie?" Nick said slowly to tease me, but I wasn't in the mood for jokes.

"I know you didn't mean to stay over. It was an accident, I get that, but I highly doubt Alisha is going to see it like that," I said carefully and watched him closely.

He seemed to tense a little, but remained still.

"Last night was a lot of fun and I really enjoy spending time with you. But I think for the sake of your relationship, we shouldn't hang out like this again. I don't want to jeopardize your future with Alisha."

"Rosie, it's okay. She'll understand. If she asks, I'll explain everything to her and she'll know it was all out of innocence. We were just friends hanging out, watching a couple of movies, right?" Nick asked, raising an eyebrow, but I shook my head.

"Friends don't sit in a car by themselves, hold hands, or have feelings for the other person." I stared at my hands, not daring to look at him.

"You have feelings… for me?"

I looked at him and didn't know what to say. I couldn't find the words. He regarded me with a look of hope and eagerness to hear my answer, but I refused to clarify what I had just revealed. "It doesn't matter, Nick. You're getting married."

I stood, feeling myself becoming emotional, and took a couple deep breaths to fight the urge to cry. "I think you better leave." I felt my lips start to quiver. The stupid breathing was not working and my emotions were getting the better of me.

Nick stood with a look of concern and slowly walked toward me. "Rosie," he said with affection, but I backed away and shook my head.

"No, Nick. We can't do this. It's too complicated. I'm not going to mess this up for you," I stated and felt tears stream down my face.

Nick stood there, watching me cry, with a pained look on his face. His arms were still slightly stretched out, and he looked like he wanted to embrace and comfort me and part of me wanted that- but I could tell he was also trying to respect my wishes. "Rosie, can you just let me talk for a minute? Let me explain," he pleaded.

Again, I shook my head. "Please leave. You're just making this harder for me. Please," I begged, but he wouldn't move. I could hardly stand staring at him anymore as I kept wiping tears off my face in an attempt to not look a mess, but it wasn't working.

"Nick, I think you better go," a voice said behind him.

I saw Lily standing there, firm and confident. She looked a lot better than I did right now. I looked back at Nick, who seemed hurt and upset, but decided to finally respect my wishes.

He lowered his arms, and strolled through the living room, opened the front door, and was gone, as if he'd never been there. My knees buckled and I knelt on the floor, put my head in my hands, and started sobbing. I felt Lily's arms wrap around me in an effort to comfort me. They helped, but didn't quite do the trick.

The only arms I wished were around me, were Nick's, but I couldn't have them. They belonged to Alisha, and I was going to have to accept that and move on.

CHAPTER 13

I didn't see or hear from Nick for the next couple of weeks. I worked almost every day at the bakery to keep busy and prevent myself from thinking about Nick, so between working and preparing to graduate, I was a busy lady.

Lily and I decided to keep the Nick-and-Rosie saga between us, and not tell my mother. And we had to talk to Troy and make sure he didn't open his big mouth either. Once that boy got talking, there was no stopping him.

Since my graduation was happening later in the week, on Thursday to be exact, Mom had me make the cookie dough for Alisha's cookies and get them cut out and put in the fridge so that they were ready to be baked. On Wednesday, she had me bake them and flood-ice all the cookies, so that they could dry the next day while we were at my graduation ceremony.

Iced sugar cookies were one of those things that were a necessary evil. They were beautiful, but took all week to complete all the steps required to finalize the details and perfect the design. My mom's plan was to finish icing and decorating the cookies on Friday and then deliver them on Saturday morning for the bridal shower. She told me I didn't have to do the delivering, which I was very grateful for.

My graduation ceremony happened on Thursday and Mom, Lily and Troy came to the ceremony. Luckily, it was shorter than I thought it was going to be, but the ceremony took a turn when I saw Nick and Alisha together, posing for graduation pictures with their families. Seeing him made my stomach churn, and once I caught up with my family, I encouraged them to leave right away.

My mom didn't understand why we had to leave so quickly and was reluctant, but once I showed Lily and Troy what I was trying to get away from, they helped me get her to leave. I was a free woman, and never had to go to school ever again, unless I wanted too, which I didn't. Even though I had graduated and finished everything, and could do anything I wanted too, I felt more lost than ever.

This didn't improve when my mother invited Lily, Troy and I over for dinner the day after my graduation. She said it was very important and that we all needed to be there. She ended up closing the bakery early, which she hardly ever did, but since the four of us were the only ones that could close, she didn't really have much choice. Troy met us at our apartment and the three of us carpooled in Lily's car to Mom's.

"I wonder what Mom wants. This isn't like her to have us all over for a formal dinner on a Friday night. I swear she called me three different times today to make sure we were all coming, which was really weird," Lily thought out loud. "Usually she just waits for us to come home on the weekend and then we can spend time with her. She was very persistent that we have dinner at the house and needed to come at six o'clock sharp."

"Didn't you say she sounded nervous on the phone?" Troy reminded her.

"Yes, she did. I forgot about that. I tried to ask her what was wrong, but she insisted on us coming and said we could talk then," Lily reiterated as she continued driving in the direction of our old childhood home.

"She seemed a little off at work too. Almost like she was

distracted. I thought she was just focused on trying to get ready for the wedding orders, but maybe it's not that. A couple weeks ago, I tried to go to the house and hang out with her. I stayed up to wait for her, but I never saw her come home. I ended up falling asleep, and the next morning she pretended like nothing was wrong. It was bizarre," I told them as I watched houses go by.

"Hmm, that is weird. She's never liked staying out late. Why didn't you tell me that before?" Lily asked, sounding frustrated that I had kept information about Mom from her.

"I kind of forgot to tell you, and then the whole Nick thing happened," I answered, and became very quiet.

After that morning Nick left, Lily and I hadn't talked much about him. I assumed she had told Troy to do the same, because he didn't bother bringing him up. I was grateful he didn't, because I was still well into my healing process.

"Have you heard from him at all?" Lily inquired casually.

"No, I haven't," I whispered and blinked away tears that wanted to escape my eyes, but I refused to let them flow.

"I'm sorry, sis," she said quietly and looked at me thoughtfully out of the rearview mirror.

"Me too, Rose. For what it's worth, I think he really liked you. Maybe more than that-"

Lily touched his arm, motioning him to stop talking. She knew any talk of Nick brought instant waterworks to my eyes.

"It's okay, guys. It just wasn't meant to be. He proposed to Alisha after all and wanted to marry her. That was his choice. I just supported him and made it easier for him in the end. I didn't want to get in the way of them being happy." My voice cracked at the end.

Troy must have heard it, because he reached back his arm and held out his hand for me to take.

"You did the right thing, Rose. We should have never encouraged it," he said regretfully and stroked the back of my hand with his thumb.

If this were any other guy, I would question this kind of physical contact. However, Troy was like the best friend and brother I never had, and it never bugged Lily. She knew he cared for me, but in a different way.

"It's okay, Troy. It was innocent. You just wanted me to be happy, and I appreciate that. It's just not my time I guess. I'll find love someday, or hopefully it will find me. I'm not in any hurry. I have my whole life to look for it. Now, I need to focus on what I want to do with my life," I lamented and then smiled at Troy.

"You'll figure it out, I have no doubt." He smiled back and took his hand back to hold Lily's, intertwining his fingers with hers.

"I hope so," I muttered and watched Lily and Troy exchange concerned glances. I hated when they worried about me. I stared out the window and remained silent the rest of the car ride.

Troy and Lily started talking about something, but I didn't care to listen or engage in the conversation. I had other things on my mind.

We pulled up to the house and there was another car in the driveway that I didn't recognized. It was a brand new Dodge truck and it stood out in comparison to the other cars on the road. None of them looked as new and nice as this truck. It was definitely designed to be a flashy car with its bright red color and big tires. Whoever drove this truck wanted to flaunt it. The question was, why was it in my mother's driveway?

"Do you guys recognize that big red truck?" I asked the two lovebirds, but they shook their heads.

"Nope, I don't," Lily answered.

Troy whistled. "I don't either, and I'm pretty sure I would remember that thing. That truck is a beaut!"

"You can stop drooling, Troy," Lily said sarcastically and parked on the road.

My mom never parked in the garage because she had her workout area set up in there, so with her car in the driveway, and that big obnoxious truck, we had to park on the road.

Troy rolled his eyes and unbuckled his seat-belt. "I save my drool for you, babe," he snickered and I pretended to gag. This was not a conversation I needed to hear between the two of them.

"And on that note, I'm out of the car." I stepped out and heard Lily unbuckle her seatbelt.

"You can keep that drool to yourself, ya nasty," Lily quipped and climbed out of the car after me.

"I was only kidding," Troy insisted, but Lily rolled her eyes at him. She seemed to do that a lot with him.

The three of us strolled to the front door and Lily knocked. "I hope y'all are ready," she muttered.

"Ready for what?" I questioned.

Just then, the door swung open and Mom answered with a man standing next to her; he was beaming with the biggest smile I'd ever seen. The guy had the whitest teeth I had ever seen, too. He was easily a head taller than my mom and had his hand comfortably resting on her shoulder. His hair was half blonde, half grey, and was starting to thin on the top, but he'd tried to cover it up with the way he'd parted his hair on the side.

Besides those sparkling white teeth, his most noticeable feature had to be his ice-blue eyes; they seemed really friendly, and had crinkles around them, which led me to believe he was a man who enjoyed life. He kind of reminded me of Donald Trump, but taller, less hair, and a lot less orange. In fact, he was paler than anyone in the room.

"Hi guys! Come on in," she beckoned and I gaped.

I couldn't believe it; Mom had a boyfriend!

The three of us walked inside, and I was instantly hit with scents of delicious food. I felt my stomach grumble and, for a moment, forgot that there was a man in my mother's kitchen, helping with dinner. I looked at the dining room table and saw that it was set with my mom's "nice" dishes. She was really going over the top.

"Why don't you guys find a seat at the table, and we'll bring the dinner over to you?" Mom suggested. "But first, Lily, will you grab the dinner rolls?"

"Sure thing, Mom" She brought the basket of rolls to the table.

"Thanks, sweetheart. I made pot roast, mashed potatoes, green beans, and a yummy cranberry and apple salad. And yes, Rosie, I made gravy, just like you like." My mom smiled and placed the gravy boat in the middle of the table. It smelled delicious.

"Thanks, Mom," I half-smiled at her and took my seat at the end of the table.

Lily and Troy sat on one side of the table and Mom and her beau stood by the side of the table; the guy had his arm around her.

"Go ahead and dig in, guys! I want to introduce this wonderful man to you. This is Hank," my mom introduced him. "Hank, this is my daughter Lily and her boyfriend, Troy. He works at the bakery with us, and this is my oldest, Rosie. Rosie is the one that graduated from college yesterday. Hank and I have been dating the last few weeks."

Hank reached out his hand to each of us and gave us a very big smile. Once the introductions were finished, Mom and Hank took their spots next to each other at the table. It was all very awkward. Clearly, my mom wasn't familiar with how to date around her children and act like a normal person.

"Nice to meet you all. I've heard a lot about you." Hank smiled cheerfully and nodded at each of us while he placed a big spoonful of gravy on his mashed potatoes.

"Funny, I haven't heard anything about you," I pointed out and leaned back in my chair and stared. I didn't like surprises.

"Oh tell us, how did you meet?" Lily shot me a warning look, and smiled at Hank.

"We actually met at that paint class I went to a couple weeks ago. As a matter of fact, he was the teacher," she informed us, smiling.

"Wow, that's awesome! So, Hank, you're an artist?" Lily asked, sounding impressed.

"Yes, part-time. I work as an attorney at a firm here in town. Painting is something I like to do in my free time. You know, something to relieve stress from the day-to-day grind," Hank explained.

"That's cool. I used to like drawing, but I haven't done it in ages," Troy piped up, and Lily seemed pleased that he wanted to join the conversation.

"Can someone please pass me the gravy?" I requested loudly so I could stop the conversation. This time, Mom gave me a look, questioning my rudeness, and passed the gravy I had asked for.

"Here you go, Rosie. Do you need anything else?" She asked me curtly.

"Nope, I think I can reach everything else. Thanks, Mom." I smiled as if nothing were wrong, plopped a big spoonful of mashed potatoes on my plate, along with a river of gravy. Then I proceeded to take a huge mouthful and smiled again.

Lily rolled her eyes and Troy looked as if he were going to bust up laughing.

"Great." My mom's mouth straightened and I knew she wasn't thrilled with me.

The rest of the conversation was all about Hank and his paintings. It was a real bore and I couldn't handle listening to it. Although, when my mom caught me looking completely unenthused, she shot a look, so I pretended that I liked hearing about Hank's artwork and his years as a painter.

Lily was super nice and asked lots of questions, Troy piped up occasionally and made some witty remarks. Me, I remained silent. I didn't like people hiding behind my back, telling secrets, and my mom had kept this one for quite some time; she was going to have to explain herself.

When Hank excused himself to go to the bathroom after we had finished eating, Mom spun her head, scowled at me, and whispered harshly, "What *is* your problem?"

"*My* problem?" I whispered in return, "You've had this super-secret boyfriend for how long? And you're *just* telling us? If anything, I have every right to have a problem!"

"Don't be so dramatic, Rosie!" she hissed. "I was worried about how you two would react and I kept putting off you two meeting him. Apparently, I had nothing to worry about," she said sarcastically, and placed a hand to her head "Can you at least pretend to be nice?"

"Well, excuse me! I feel like all you have been sneaking behind my back with all your relationships. First, I found out about Lily and Troy a couple weeks ago and they had been dating for almost a month when I found out-"

"Hey, don't bring us into this," Lily retorted quietly, cutting me off, but I ignored her.

"Now you, Mom? I feel like you all are trying to put this big bubble around me and have to lie to protect me," I used air quotes. Lily hated it when I did that, "And I hate it. I'm an adult, I can handle these things, and I would much rather you people be upfront about what is going on with you guys than keeping me in the dark… especially when you have new men in your lives! It's a *big* deal!"

"You're one to talk," Lily muttered and I glared at her with every angry bone in my body.

"Excuse me?" I tilted my head and narrowing my eyes.

"We aren't the only ones who have been keeping secrets. You've been hiding that thing about Nick from Mom this whole time," she called out, completely throwing me under the bus.

I wanted to throw my cup in her face. "That's different. We were never together; it was that one night and then, after that, I told him we shouldn't hang out like that anymore! It's not like he's some significant other in my life… like Troy or Hank!" I glanced over at my mom and she looked as if wheels were turning in her head.

"Nick who?" she whispered, and then the light bulb went off. "Oh no, you're *not* talking about Alisha's..."

"Yep, that Nick," Lily clarified, and now I wanted to throw my cup *and* plate at her.

"You went out with Nick? He's practically married!" my mom shrieked, but before anything else could be said, Hank walked back into the dining room and sat down.

"Well, should we clear the table and get the dessert ready?" he asked her, and she put on her best fake smile.

She was clearly caught off guard, but did her best to hide it from Hank. "Yes, that sounds like a great idea." She grinned and leaned close, muttering low enough so only I could hear. "Getting the knives off the table is probably a wise decision."

I rolled my eyes and stood, and picked up my dishes to rinse off in the sink. Troy rose behind me and followed to do the same, and then Lily.

I turned around and looked at my sister to glare at her, but she refused to meet my eyes. I returned to the table and waited for Mom to bring the dessert. Usually, I would offer my help, but I was in no mood to be around my family at the moment. Unfortunately, that meant I was sharing the table with Hank for the moment.

"So, Rosie, what are your plans now that you've graduated?" He asked.

I hated this question. "I don't know. I figure I'll continue working with Mom at the bakery and transfer to full-time, so she could focus more on her own full-time job. I've also been throwing around the idea of traveling around Europe a little bit," I told him, and this seemed to catch the attention of everyone else.

"Wait, what?" my mom asked.

"Yeah, I've never heard you mention this," Lily added.

"Well, you've never asked," I shot back. "I've been thinking about giving myself my own little graduation present and traveling around Europe. Maybe take a few pastry classes in France. Eat some delicious pizza in Italy."

"When do you think you'll go?" my mom asked with a creased brow.

I took a deep breath, "Well, I was thinking of going shortly after Nick and Alisha's wedding. I know you need my help with it, so I wasn't wanting to leave before that."

"And you're going to go by yourself?" she questioned, clearly trying to process what I've told her.

"Yes, I am. Who else is going to come with me? I don't have a Troy or a Hank to go with me."

After I made that comment, Lily and Mom shifted uncomfortably in their seats. Hank looked over at my mom with a confused expression and Troy looked guilty.

"I want to go, and do something fun, before I start working so much."

"We'll talk about this some more later; in the meantime, let's eat some cake. I'm playing with a new cake flavor that I want you all to try." She started cutting into the cake and served us all slices.

"Sweet! I love trying new flavors!" Troy said excitedly, trying to lighten the mood.

"I didn't know you were recipe testing, Mom. What flavor is this?" Lily asked, examining her slice. "It smells really good."

"This is a raspberry-lemon cake with a shortbread crust. It's a lemon cake with raspberry frosting and shortbread crumble inside the cake filling for texture," she explained and took a bite. "And frosted with a torched meringue. I wanted something that resembled the taste of a tart, but in cake form. I had a similar dessert like this when I went out with Hank the other night. It was my inspiration."

I took a bite and was surprised by the amount of flavor; the tartness from the lemon, sweetness from the raspberry frosting and the shortbread crumble gave it a fun texture from an otherwise soft cake. It was quite delicious. "Mom, this is really good. I love the shortbread crust. It helps tone down the sweetness."

"Me too. This raspberry buttercream is delicious. Probably one of my favorites you've made," Lily complimented her taking another bite. The frosting had always been her favorite part of cake.

"Well done, Karen," Hank also praised her as he squeezed her hand. "I think this is the best cake I've ever had."

"I hear that! Can I have another slice?" Troy asked innocently.

I snorted and took another bite. Classic Troy.

"You sure can. I certainly can't eat this whole cake," my mom responded, slicing another piece for him.

"Well, my dear, I would love to stay for another piece, but I better be going. Thank you so much for inviting me for dinner… it was all delicious and it was wonderful to meet the three of you." He smiled and gave my mom a kiss on the cheek, which sent my skin crawling.

"Let me walk you to the door," she offered and stood to lead him to the front door.

Once they were out of the room, I took the opportunity to jump on my sister. "What was all that about? I thought we were going to keep the whole Nick situation a secret! You totally threw me under the bus! And in front of Hank nonetheless! That was the most awkward dinner of my life."

"You threw me and Troy under the bus too!" Lily retorted, but I waved her off.

"Yours was not as big of a deal as mine! Nick is a married man and a client to Mom! You and Troy dating is not as big of a deal as the me-and-Nick thing," I complained and pushed my cake away. I wasn't in the mood to eat anymore.

"Well, she needed to know. We shouldn't keep things from her," Lily argued, clearly becoming more upset and I noticed Troy rested his hand on her thigh to comfort her.

"That wasn't your thing to share! I was planning on telling

her. I was just trying to give myself a little more time to get over it and think of how to explain it," I rattled on, exasperated. "Don't you realize I'm still trying to move past the whole thing! It wasn't easy for me and I'm still struggling. I saw the dumb guy at the graduation ceremony, being cozy with Alisha, and taking pictures with each other and their families. And it hurt.

"I like a guy who's planning on getting married in what, a week now? The sad part is that I just don't like him. I *really* like him, and I had to tell him I didn't want to see him anymore, which is the last thing I wanted to tell him. And then you go and shoot your mouth off to Mom!" I stopped talking, because I felt myself becoming way too emotional, and forced myself to get under control.

"Rosie, I'm sorry. I had no idea." Lily appeared overwhelmed by guilt.

"No, you didn't. But then again, I don't understand why it's something you couldn't figure out on your own," I shot at her and crossed my arms.

Lily looked down and didn't know what to say. An awkward silence fell over the table, until Mom walked back in, looking as frustrated as I'd ever seen her.

"Okay, you guys, what is going on? Rosie, you have a lot of explaining to do and no one is leaving until I get answers."

"Do I have to talk about this right now? I really don't want to," I admitted and put my head in my hands and stared at the table.

"Fine, if you won't, can Lily tell me?" she requested and waited for me to respond.

I simply nodded my head, and heard Mom's voice directed at Lily. "Alright Lily, spill."

Lily took a deep breath and started telling her everything that had happened between me and Nick- with Troy's help too, since most of the time when I was with Nick, Troy happened to be there.

She started with the first time he entered the bakery, the

grocery store, the party where I punched Jake, when Nick found me at the café, and we went to the drive-thru movie, and then everything that happened at our apartment.

I looked up now and again, at my mom to watch her facial expressions, and her looks ranged from shock to surprise to confusion. There were seconds when she appeared upset, but she quickly shook off the visible dismay; I believed she thought if we knew she was upset, we would stop telling her everything, or at least cut down the amount of details.

When Lily finished telling everything, Mom took a deep breath and leaned back in her chair. "So, this has all been happening for the last few weeks, and you haven't said anything? Why?" She looked at me, her forehead crinkled with concern and confusion.

I sighed, exasperated. "Because I didn't want you to worry or stress. He's a client and I didn't want you to think that I was trying to ruin this big order for you." I looked at the table, not wanting to look at Mom's face.

Unexpectedly, I felt a warm hand touch mine and I saw that Mom was smiling. "Rosie, I know you would never do that. It sounds like everything that happened was innocent, besides Troy inviting Nick to the movies and you four inadvertently having a double date!"

She spun her head to look at Troy and he sunk in his seat and scanned the ceiling, clearly feeling guilty. "All of it sounds like he sought you out and genuinely wanted to be around you, Rosie. There's nothing you could have done, except for what you did do, and that was telling him you guys couldn't hang out anymore. I can't imagine how hard it must have been for you, and I have a lot of respect for you for doing that."

She squeezed my hand encouragingly and I gave her a little smile. "Thanks, Mom."

"So, I just have to clarify, to truly make sense of all of this, do you like him?" she asked hesitantly and regarded me closely.

I nodded. "Yes."

"And this may be a stupid question, but does *he* like *you*?"

Lily ended up answering for me and snorted, "Oh yes, Mom. He's head-over-heels for her."

I watched our mom's lips purse and she sat in her chair for a full moment and stared at me, deep in thought. She let go of my hand and clasped her own hands and twirled her thumbs. "Rosie, what do you want to do about the wedding this upcoming week? I not only have the cake to worry about, but I also have the pastries to make for the brunch earlier that morning. If you don't want to be a part of this wedding, I understand."

I shook my head. "No. If I don't, it will look weird. Alisha and Nick are expecting me to be there with you, helping out. If I don't show up, they're going to know something is up. I need to see this thing through to the end. There's going to be lots of times when I'm going to have to work with a client I don't want too, and I'll need to suck it up. This will just be good practice."

"You're calling this practice? It sounds more like torture to me," Troy deadpanned, crossing his arms.

Lily nudged his arm and shot him a dirty look.

Mom ignored him and looked at me. "As long as you're sure, we'll continue to prepare for the wedding. We have a lot to do next week."

"I'm sure, Mom. I'm not going to leave you behind… that wouldn't be right." I tried to sound certain, but I could hear doubt in my own voice.

"Okay," she said and gave me a smile. "It's all going to be okay. Now, when were you going to tell me about this trip to Europe?"

"I don't know. After that whole thing with Nick and the graduation ceremony yesterday, I figured now would be as good a time as any to take the opportunity to do some traveling before I commit to the bakery full time," I stated.

"And are you really planning on going alone?" she inquired, looking displeased.

I shrugged. "I guess. I mean, I thought about asking you or Lily to come with me, but I already knew your answer."

"You know I can't leave the bakery for that long," Mom confirmed.

"And I'm taking summer classes, and I need to work to be able to pay for them and keep up on rent. How do you plan on paying for this trip and being able to keep up your part of the bills?" Lily wondered aloud, tilting her head to the side with one eyebrow raised.

"Lily, do you realize *how much* I actually work? I worked almost full-time the entire time I was at school. I received scholarships for my grades, which took care of tuition, and I worked a lot in high school... not to mention, I haven't done traveling, I hardly go out or eat out, and I haven't had a boyfriend to spend my money on, no offense," I offered matter-of-factly.

"None taken," she mumbled.

"Having us live together and splitting the rent actually helped a lot and I've been able to save a lot of money. Enough to where I can still keep up my side of the bills, pay for a very comfortable trip to Europe, and still have a chunk of savings when I come back," I finished and looked at her a little smugly.

Lily sat silently for a moment and pondered on my words. "I guess you're right; you've pretty much had no life except for school and Mom's bakery- well, besides Nick. You've got to admit that was a nice change of pace," she teased and I rolled my eyes.

"Be nice, Lil," our mom warned.

"I'm just saying." She held up her hands in surrender and stopped talking.

"Well, we'll talk about this more after the wedding and figure out the details. I don't like the idea of you going to Europe alone, so maybe we can figure out a different option," Mom conceded and sliced another piece of cake. "Anyone else want another one?" Troy raised his hand eagerly and Lily pushed her plate over to Mom.

"Alright, Mom, your turn. What's up with Hank?" I asked casually.

"Yeah! How serious is this? I thought you were never going to date another man again," Lily pointed out and took a big bite of cake.

Mom instantly blushed and started twirling her hair like a little schoolgirl. "That was *before* I met Hank. He was so kind to me when I went to that class and gave me lots of helpful hints. I actually want to use the skills I learned in painting class and start painting cakes with edible coloring. I think it would be so pretty and a fun thing to add to my repertoire.

"Anyways, after a class, he asked to walk me to my car. Then, once he'd done that, he asked me out to dinner that Friday night, and from there, we've gone out multiple times a week. He's visited me at the bakery and even brought me breakfast when I would go in early in the morning."

"Really? I never even noticed him," I sputtered and looked at Lily, and by the look on her face, she had never noticed either.

"Oh, I made sure he never came when you girls were there. I didn't want to introduce him to you guys, unless I knew it was serious," she explained and intwined her fingers again, twirling her thumbs.

"Well, apparently, it's serious now if you're introducing us," Lily pointed out as she flipped her hair back.

"Yes, it is. I guess you could say now that he's my boyfriend, which sounds completely juvenile, but probably more accurate than anything else. I don't know... he makes me really happy, and I want to see where things go with him. Now, I understand if this makes you girls uncomfortable. I know I haven't had a man in my life for quite some time, so I'm sure you two have some mixed feelings." She was eyeing me closely and, I couldn't blame her; I'd been a beast at dinner.

"I'm sorry for how I acted. I want you to be happy, so if Hank makes you happy, then I'm happy. Just as long as he's good to you and treats you right." I smiled encouragingly and she smiled back.

"Thank you, Rosie. That means a lot." Still smiling, she turned to Lily. "And you, miss?"

"I echo what Rosie said. If you're happy, I'm happy. Plus, it seems like he can take care of you just fine. An attorney and a painter. That sounds pretty dreamy, Mom," she winked and our mom giggled like a little schoolgirl.

"He sure is. Well thank you guys for all coming over, but I think it was a well needed dinner- even though it was incredibly awkward. And now, all the secrets are out, I hope." She hesitated and looked at Troy. "You've been unusually quiet tonight, Troy. Do you have anything you need to say?" She teased and everyone laughed, except for him.

He just smiled and nodded.

After the laughter died down, he spoke. "Actually, now that you mention it, Karen, I do have something to say. I'm in love with your daughter," he confessed and regarded Lily. "I love you, Lily. I can't imagine my life without you and I know we haven't been dating for very long, but I've known you for a long time, and you've always been there for me. Listening to your mom talk about Hank just made me realize… that I love you."

"Troy, that is so sweet. I love you too," Lily proclaimed and wrapped her arms around his neck and kissed him.

Mom and I exchanged glances, and then started laughing. This had been quite an eventful dinner and my emotions had been through enough. After Troy and Lily expressed their love to each other, right in front of us, we helped Mom clean the kitchen, and then drove back to the apartment.

Troy and Lily dropped me off, and they went off to talk, but I highly doubted there would be any talking going on. I walked into the apartment feeling very alone. As I looked around, I reflected on what had happened not minutes before. My mom had a boyfriend, Troy and Lily were in love, and I was alone and had no idea what I wanted to do with my life. Other than my intentions of working at the bakery, I didn't have much planned after that- I was a college graduate with no plans and no strings attached to anything. My classmates were moving forward with careers and their loved ones, and I was left with no one. What was I supposed to do now?

SUGAR COOKIE RECIPE

1 ½ cups unsalted butter
2 cups sugar
2 room temperature eggs
1 tsp. salt
4 tsps. baking powder
5-6 cups flour (plus more for rolling out dough)
1 cup milk
2 tsps. vanilla

1. Preheat oven to 375 degrees.
2. Cream together butter and sugar.
3. Add eggs and cream until light and fluffy.
4. Mix in salt, baking powder, and enough flour until it's not sticking to the sides of the bowl. Do not over mix.
5. Add milk and vanilla.
6. Chill dough for approximately two hours.
7. Roll out and cut cookies into desired shapes.
8. Bake for 8-10 minutes.

CHAPTER 14

With Nick and Alisha's wedding happening just around the corner, Mom and I were doing a mad dash to finish everything. This was a big client for my mother and she wanted to make sure everything was perfect.

Not only did we have a huge wedding cake to make, she had a brunch to cater on the same day. It was an important week for her, and I wanted to support her as much as possible, but there was a big part of me that didn't want to have anything to do with this wedding. I'd been tempted to tell her that I couldn't help her out with this one, but I knew she would come apart if I told her that. I was her right-hand man, and I couldn't bail on her. Not with the wedding just days away.

Mom put me in charge of sugar flowers, which took a lot of time to create. Alisha wanted a lot of flowers on the cake, especially roses, which required that numerous individual petals be cut and rolled out.

It took me a couple of days to do all the cut outs. Then, it took another day to dry the flowers so that they became rock hard and, once they were rock hard, they were ready to be colored with edible colored dust the next day. She wanted the flowers to be blush pink, just like from the tasting, and all the leaves to be a dark leafy green. This took a long time to dust and Lily offered to come help dust the flowers because, on Friday, our mom wanted to put the cake together, which included placing the flowers on the cake.

While I was working on making those sugar flowers, Mom and Troy had been baking the cakes, preparing the filling and icing, and covering each tier in fondant for a clean white look. This took all week to do between baking, cooking fillings, stacking, crumb coating each cake, icing and covering them in fondant. It was a good thing we'd planned on taking a week to make this cake, with all the tiers Alisha had wanted. She'd ended up deciding on the white cake, with the raspberry filling and vanilla buttercream; she'd insisted those were the perfect flavors for a wedding cake.

She'd also been dead set on having six tiers with gum paste ruffles on the bottom, quilted beading on the second tier, edible lace on the third, a bunch of roses on the fourth. The fifth would have lattice piping that Mom would hand-pipe. The top tier, which would be plain white, would be mostly covered in the blush roses, along with other roses bunched together here and there. It was going to be beautiful, no doubt, but it was a lot of hard work to be done, which was why we needed an entire week.

Come Thursday, Mom had started working on the decorations on the individual tiers and finished them Friday; she was then ready to place the roses.

When we weren't working on the cake, we were busting out cinnamon rolls, muffins and scones. Mom made this Lily's job and when we were waiting on something to dry or to set, we would jump in and help her make the dough and keep things coming in and out of the oven. Luckily, my mom had a big one, so we could bake on multiple racks, but it still was a lot of food to keep up on. Apparently, there were a lot of people invited to this brunch, and even more were invited to the wedding; Alisha had estimated about three hundred people for the wedding and that was *after* cutting down the guest list. I didn't even know that many people, let alone have that many people in my close circle.

On Friday, once my mom finished decorating all the cakes, she began the final details along with stacking the cakes, and I helped Lily with the last of the baked goods. I iced cinnamon rolls, glazed lemon-poppyseed muffins, and drizzled dark chocolate on the raspberry scones. Once everything was finished, we boxed up the delicious goodies and set them aside so that they were ready to deliver in the morning. Right before closing time, Mom finished placing the gum paste roses, and stared at her finished product.

"The great cake is finally finished," Troy declared dramatically and the three of us laughed.

"Leave it to you to come up with something 'witty'," I said drolly.

"That's what I'm here for," he chuckled and I laughed at him.

"It's a beautiful cake, Mom. You did an amazing job," Lily complimented and wrapped an arm around her.

"It wasn't just me. We all chipped in. Rosie, you did an awesome job with the roses. They look so real," she smiled praising me. "You've really come a long way in your sugar work."

"Thanks, Mom. I just hope Alisha likes it. *She's* the one we have to impress," I replied grudgingly and Troy smirked.

"I'm sure she'll love it," Lily stated encouragingly. "You worry too much about what that chick thinks."

"Well, she *is* the one paying for all of this and it is her special day, so yes, I'm worried what she's going to think. The last thing I want to do is tick her off," I admitted and walked around the cake to give it a closer inspection.

"I doubt she's going to hate it, Rosie. It's the prettiest wedding cake I've ever seen," Troy told me and wrapped an arm around my shoulders. "Besides, if she *really* doesn't like it, at least she'll know it tastes good."

I looked up at him and rolled my eyes, "You kill me."

He then wrapped the other arm around me and squeezed me in a tight hug, "Oh, I think someone is a little tired. Maybe we should all go out to eat? I could go for some food."

"Oh, yeah, I could definitely eat," Lily agreed and looked at Mom. "Do you want to come?"

"No, I don't think I'm going to, but maybe next time. I think Hank is wanting to get together tonight," she declined as she took off her apron.

"Well, you have fun with that. Girls, let's go get some food! I'm feeling Mexican; what do you think?" Troy asked, and put his other arm around Lily so that we both had an arm around us. He probably felt like such a stud.

"I was hoping you would say that," Lily said excitedly, and started jumping up and down. "I've been craving Mexican food! And, I think, it's karaoke night, so we can listen to some awful music too." She giggled excitedly and I laughed. She thought I was laughing at her joke, but really, I was just laughing at her, because of how excited she always got over Mexican food.

"I could go for chips and salsa," I nodded and grabbed my bag as we walked out the door. "See you bright and early tomorrow, Mom!" I called over my shoulder.

I heard her call back, "See you in the morning, Rose!"

The restaurant was on the same street as the bakery, so we only had to walk a couple blocks. As we approached, we started hearing mariachi music. Lily and Troy walked hand in hand in front of me, and I trailed behind, feeling like the biggest third wheel ever.

We entered the restaurant and were consumed by the Mexican atmosphere. Many conversations were transpiring, so the noise level was high. Mariachi music played in the background and television screens showed baseball games above the long bar. The heavy, wonderful smells of Mexican food overwhelmed me; my stomach rumbled and I was ready to dig into nacho chips and salsa.

They showed us to a booth in the corner where we had a

good view of everything, so it was great for people watching. I sat on one side by myself, and Lily and Troy sat on the other side, snuggling up. If I didn't like them so much, they would drive me crazy… more than usual.

The waitress came around to give us menus and ask what we wanted to drink, and then left quickly to see to another table. Fridays were clearly very popular to go out because they had people in the restaurant sitting so close, everyone was squished together like sardines.

The waitress returned with our drinks; I always chose water while my sister and Troy preferred soda, and she gave us the requested chips and salsa. As for our orders, I always picked a tamale and an enchilada, Lily chose shrimp fajitas, and Troy went with a massive pork burrito. The moment the waitress left the table, I started devouring the chips and salsa. I hadn't realized how hungry I was, but Troy had been spot on.

Besides the smoothie run Troy had done around breakfast time, I had mostly eaten the baked goods we had made in the bakery, in addition to tasting multiple frostings to make sure they were right; other than that, I hadn't eaten much of anything else.

"Geez, Rose, I think we should have gotten an extra basket of chips and salsa just for you," Troy teased and laughed at his own joke. He tended to do that a lot.

"It's my kryptonite," I shrugged and picked up another chip. "You know I love these… plus, I'm hungry!"

"Cleary," Lily snorted. "Oh, our food is coming. Troy, take those chips away from her or she won't eat her dinner," she joked and Troy yanked away the basket of chips.

I stuck my tongue out at her, which made me feel a little juvenile, and quickly pulled it back in when the waitress arrived. She placed our dishes in front of us, and let us know the plates were hot before walking away. My hunger took over and I dug into the enchilada. When I came up for air, I gazed at Lily and Troy;

they seemed just as hungry as I was because half their plates were gone.

"So, next time, let's not let ourselves get this hungry again because, Troy, that burrito was as big as your face, and you've demolished it, no problem," I giggled.

Lily waved a finger and swallowed. "No, that's just him. Troy eats more than anyone I've ever met."

"Are you calling me a pig?" asked Troy accusingly.

"Would I be wrong?" Lily shot back, giggling.

Troy shrugged. "No, probably not." He returned to the burrito.

"Me, on the other hand, I'm getting full, but these are so good! Too bad Mexican food is never as good the next day," she moaned and stared at her food, debating whether or not to eat it all or just give up.

"Yeah, I'm slowing down too. I feel like those chips are expanding in my stomach. I ate way too many," I admitted and leaned back in my seat.

"You do this all the time." Lily shook her head and picked at the shrimp in her meal. This usually meant she wasn't going to take it home, so she wanted to eat the good parts while still hot and yummy.

"I know," I moaned. "I haven't even touched my tamale. At least tamales aren't as bad the next morning." I gazed around for the waitress and waved her over to ask for a box.

I noticed someone familiar at the front, being led to a table by the hostess. When I realized who it was, I pressed myself against the wall as quickly as I could and lowered my head.

"Uh, Rosie, what are you doing?" Lily asked, raising an eyebrow.

"Yeah, you look like you've seen a ghost," Troy piped in.

"Oh no, this person is alive and quite well," I said sarcastically and the two of them looked at me quizzically.

"Rose, *who* did you see?" Lily asked, gazing casually around the room.

"You would never guess," I muttered and pressed fingers to my temples as I felt a headache coming on.

"Okay, now I have to know." Troy peered around the booth and, groaned, "I can't see anyone we know. Especially not like this."

"Rosie, will you just tell us who it was you saw?" Lily asked pointedly, clearly impatient.

"Fine." I took a deep breath and whispered, "It was Nick."

"What!" Lily's eyes grew wide and searched the restaurant more aggressively.

"Lily, stop it," I squeaked. "If he sees you, he's going to come over here for sure."

"What are the odds of him being in the same restaurant as us, before his wedding day?" Asked Troy quietly and tapped Lily lightly on the shoulder."Do you see him?"

"Troy," I said, exasperated. "Come on!"

"What? I'm just curious. Can you blame me?" Troy smiled mischievously.

"Uh, yes, I can!" I waved a hand at him and took a calming breath. "I really don't want him to see me here. He needs to get married tomorrow, and then we can all move on!"

"Oh, crap." Lily exhaled sharply and turned around, looking scared.

"What?" I asked, my eyes rounding with fear.

"He may have seen me. I don't know! The hostess is leading them over here… I think… to the booth behind us," Lily shrieked and shifted from the edge of her seat.

I bent across the table to whisper something, then caught a glimpse of the hostess, quickly grabbed the drink menu and held it over my face.

I heard her ask with a heavy accent, "Is this booth going to be okay?" It was clear her first language had been Spanish.

"Yes, this is great, thank you," Nick's deep voice replied and I heard people sit down.

Once the hostess walked away, I slowly put down my menu

and looked up cautiously to make sure I couldn't see anyone- and they couldn't see me.

When the coast was clear, I glared at Lily.

"What?" she whispered. "It's not like I told her to come sit Nick right behind us!"

"You may as well have," I whispered angrily in return.

Lily pouted and narrowed her eyes. "No, I didn't!"

"What are we supposed to do now? We can't leave the booth without him seeing us!" I was seething and crossed my arms.

"Listen, we can figure this out," Troy interrupted our bickering. "It's not as big of a deal if he sees me and Lily… it's you we have to sneak out of here. Maybe me and Lily can get up first, block the view, and then you can slip away."

"That's probably our best bet," I agreed and groaned. "Why me?" I shook my head and then my ears picked up on Nick's voice, deep in conversation. I stopped and noticed that had heard him too.

"Whoa, man, what are you talking about?"

"Yeah, I'm confused, man. What about Alisha? I thought you, like, loved her," Asked another deep voice.

"I know, I know," Noah piped up. "I'm just not feeling it as much as I used to. Besides, I feel like- lately she's just not into us anymore, maybe just the *idea* of us. I feel terrible even saying this… but sometimes I feel like I'm just another business transaction for her family and they're ensuring she's going to have a nice life because she's marrying me."

"You mean, like, she's just marrying you for your money and your place in your dad's company?" Nick's companion clarified.

"Yes." Nick grew quiet for a bit and then groaned. "Doesn't that sound terrible? At one point in our relationship, I could tell you without a shadow of a doubt that I loved her, and I knew that she loved me, which is why I proposed. But now…"

"You don't know if you two are in love anymore," the guy finished Nick's thought and Nick must have done something to confirm his thoughts, because the guy then said, "Dang, I'm sorry, man."

"What are you going to do? I mean, your wedding is tomorrow."

Nick didn't get a chance to answer because the waiter strolled past with water and chips and salsa. They started eating and talking about what they were going to order instead of the wedding and I turned my attention to Lily and Troy.

They had to be mimicking my own expression, because they appeared to be in complete disbelief and shock.

"You guys have got to get me out of here," I urged and Lily looked at me quizzically.

"Are you serious? Don't you want to know what else he's going to say next?" she asked and I shook my head.

"No, I can't bear it. I need you to get me out of here, *right now*, please!" I begged and Troy looked sympathetic.

"We'll get you out, Rose." He smiled and turned to Lily. "You're going to stand up, face away from him, and I'm going to stand up by you, but we're not going to move until Rose gets up-so she can escape *very* quickly." He reached into his back pocket, pulled out money and placed it on the table. "Forty should be enough for all of us and tip, right?"

"Um, that's plenty," Lily replied, looking frustrated by the amount he placed on the table, but she wasn't going to bring it up now. "Are we ready? Rose, do you have your phone and car keys?"

I nodded."I'm ready to go." My stomach felt like it was in knots, but adrenaline was running through me, so I was ready to exit as soon as Lily stood.

"Okay, Lily, go," Troy said solemnly and she jumped up, making sure her back was directly behind the booth.

Troy quickly slid out and stood by her and jumped up and walked away, never looking back. I waited outside for Lily and Troy.

Some five minutes later, Lily and Troy stepped through the

door with looks of relief on their faces. "Well, he noticed us and said hi, but he never said anything about you, so I think my plan worked," Troy said looking pumped.

Lily rolled her eyes, giggling. "He did look a little embarrassed, though. I think he may have realized that we probably heard him talking about Alisha, but other than that, he was nice. He asked if we were going to be at the wedding tomorrow, helping with Mom, but I told him it was just going to be you with her. He seemed very happy about that." She winked and this time I rolled my eyes.

"I highly doubt that. I haven't spoken to him in weeks," I said grudgingly. "I'm going home. I have an interesting day ahead tomorrow and I need to try and sleep."

"Let me know how it goes tomorrow. I'm curious to hear," teased Lily.

"Maybe you should just come and see how it goes," I offered and started backing away.

Lily shook her head. "No thanks. Me and Troy are going to open up the bakery for a bit, and then Mom gave us permission to close around lunch so that we can spend the rest of the day together."

"Well, you have fun with that. See you later." I waved and walked to my car.

Once I was home, I did my best to sleep, but I could not shut my mind off. I lay in bed and stared at the ceiling, dreading going to work the next day, watching a guy that I liked marry another woman. The sad thing, at dinner, when I heard his voice, I realized just how much I really liked him- and it was more than I realized.

CHAPTER 15

I woke up to the sound of the alarm going off in my ear. I must have fallen asleep looking at my phone because it was still in my bed. I didn't sleep nearly as much as I should have. I'd tossed and turned all night with my thoughts going a million miles an hour and had nightmares when I did manage to sleep.

I sat up in the bed and felt like I had been hit by a bus. My mind seemed groggy, my head hurt, and my body felt completely limp, not at all refreshed like it should have been after a night of fitful sleep. I didn't know how I was going to survive the day with Nick's wedding.

Mom and I had decided to meet at the bakery at seven to get everything loaded up and ready to go. Our goal was to be at Nick's house by eight. Apparently, in the back, on the patio, was where they were setting up for the brunch, and eating at ten. Mom wanted to make sure we had plenty of time to deliver the food and set up the pastries. Since we were delivering the cake, we would be driving nice and slowly to avoid having the cake topple over. Unfortunately, with the extra allotted time we were giving ourselves, this meant more time at Nick's house and around the happy couple, which I was not looking forward to.

I decided to take a short run to clear my thoughts and wake from my daze. The morning air was crisp and cool, which helped jog my foggy brain. The leaves and grass glistened with droplets of dew that had formed early in the morning. The sun was poking out from the trees, which created a beautiful sunrise that cast shadows around my feet. The air was cool enough to be comfortable after my body warmed up from running for five minutes. I wasn't a fast runner by any means, but I enjoyed the exercise and the freedom to be able to go wherever I wanted to on my very own two feet.

The run did just what I needed it to; I felt like a big weight had been lifted off my shoulders and I was much more clear-headed. I came back home and noticed the apartment was still quiet, so I did my best to keep the noise level to a minimum and snuck into the bathroom to shower unnoticed.

I took a little more effort in getting ready, since I was going to a wedding… and I may have been trying to impress someone subconsciously. I spent a little extra time applying makeup and took the time to blow dry and curl my hair to create soft beach waves.

I emerged from the bathroom after being in there for ninety minutes, and found Lily on the couch, staring at her phone.

"Good morning, sis," I said, leaned against the doorframe, and crossed my arms to wait for an answer.

"Morning." She looked at me and her mouth dropped. "Holy crap, Rose, I haven't seen you get that ready in years, if ever," she pointed out and I frowned. "What? It's true." She held up her hands defensively.

"It's a wedding. A very expensive wedding. The least I could do is get ready for it. Don't read anything into it," I barked and stalked into my room.

"Whatever you say," she called back.

I thought about letting it go, but wasn't in a forgiving mood, so I walked back out into the living room. "Lily, this day is going to be hard enough as it is, so can you please just support me and not make this any harder on me than it needs to be? I already don't want to do this, and I'm only doing it for Mom," I explained and tilted my head as I eyed her. "Got it?"

"Yes, Rosie!" She waved me off. "I support you. You happy?" she asked cheekily.

I rolled my eyes in response and walked back into my room, where I stared at the clothes in my closet, deciding what to wear. Mom liked it when we wore a little uniform, so I decided on skinny black trousers, a white blouse with flutter sleeves, and pink stiletto heels. I loved taking the opportunity to use shoes to bring in pops of color.

Once I was completely dressed, I returned to the living room and found Lily sipping water. When she looked at me, she choked on it and started coughing. "Holy crap Rose, you look like you're out for revenge. You look hot," she sputtered and eyed me up and down. "When did you get those heels? They're adorable. No one is going to be looking at the bride while you're there. Nick doesn't stand a chance!"

"So, are you saying I should change my shoes?" I asked wryly and walked over to get myself a drink of water.

"No! Don't change a thing; you look awesome. I can't wait to hear all about it," Lily said excitedly. "Troy and I are going on a hike, then out to dinner, and maybe catching a movie afterwards. Then, I'll get to come home and hear all about your time at the wedding. This is going to be the best day ever!" She clapped excitedly, but I wasn't nearly as enthused as my little sister.

"I'm so glad you're enjoying yourself," I said sarcastically. "Have a good day with Troy. I'm going to head to the bakery. I'm a little later than I wanted to be."

"That's because you decided to be a knockout for the wedding and spend more time in the bathroom than you ever have," she joshed, but I decided to ignore it and grabbed my purse, phone and keys.

"Aren't you supposed to be going to the bakery to, you

know, work? Because Mom and I are going to be at the wedding?" I hinted and raised an eyebrow curiously at her.

"I'm coming behind you. I accidentally slept through my alarm clock and let Mom know, and she said it wasn't a big deal because she was already at the bakery and had opened it. Troy got there on time. Don't worry. He's been giving me a hard time for it," Lily informed me and I started laughing.

"Wow. You slept in and you're letting Mom and your boyfriend do all your work. That's a new low," I teased.

Lily shot me a look and then glared. "You mean as bad as being in love with someone who's getting married to another woman today?"

"I am not in love with him," I declared.

"Yeah, sure, I believe that. Let me know how today goes when you see him standing at the end of the aisle, waiting for his beautiful bride to walk down it in front of all their family and friends," she stated flatly.

"Goodbye, Lily" I yelled and marched to the front door.

"Knock 'em dead" she called after me.

I shut the door before I could entertain the thought of saying something else.

I entered the bakery and was welcomed by Troy's wary face.

"Thank heaven you're here," he mumbled.

"Why? What's wrong?" I asked, setting my keys on the counter.

"Your mom is a basket case. I've never seen her this nervous," he answered warily and looked behind his shoulder to make sure she wasn't in earshot. "I walked in and she was pacing the store, muttering to herself. She looked upset. Then, when she realized I'd seen her, she put on this charade and pretended to be happy and greet me. But then, once she was done saying her pleasantries, she went into the back and didn't come out. She keeps muttering to herself too."

"Okay, I'll go back there. Wish me luck," I said unenthusiastically and took a deep breath before strolling into the back. I peered around the corner and saw Mom staring at the wedding cake, as if she wanted to push it over.

"Hey, Mom," I greeted hesitantly. "How are you doing?"

"I'd be doing a lot better if your sister bothered to show up on time," she snapped, which wasn't like her at all.

"She told me she was on her way when I left; she'll be here soon. What else is going on?" I asked tentatively, and looked behind me to see Troy was leaning up against the wall, watching the conversation go down, but tucked away where Mom couldn't see him.

"What do you mean?" I snapped my head back in her direction and found her pacing in front of the cake. "This cake is hideous. Alisha is going to completely hate it. And we're already going in there on pins and needles, because you decided to have a little fling with the groom!"

If this were anyone else, I would bark back and put that person in their place, but this was my mother. I had to have more respect. Given this was not her usual behavior and there was more to the store, I walked over, put my arms around her, and gave her a hug. She immediately relaxed and wrapped her arms around me and sighed heavily. "Mom, what's wrong? This cake is the most beautiful cake you have ever made. I don't think it's possible for anyone to hate this cake, so what's going on?"

"It's Hank. I called him last night, asking if he wanted to go out to eat and he made some excuse that he couldn't. I tried to call him a couple of times over the week and he's been ignoring my calls. I just don't know what I did wrong or why he's not answering me," she explained quietly. She pulled away and sat down, wiping her curly hair out of her eyes. She hadn't yet put on any makeup, which worried me a little, because our plan was to leave in less than an hour.

"I'm sorry, Mom. I'm sure there is some valid reason why he hasn't gotten a hold of you. I wouldn't stress too much about it.

Guys aren't the best when it comes to communication. Are they, Troy?" I said loud enough to make a point, to know that I knew he was listening.

Obviously he'd heard me, because he chuckled and walked into the room.

"Yeah, and we don't mean anything by it. We're just boys who get easily distracted. I wouldn't worry about it, Karen," he assured her and smiled.

"Really?" She looked hopeful. "You really think it's probably nothing?"

"Mom, he was completely head-over-heels at dinner, I wouldn't worry about it. In the meantime, we have a big job to do today. No offense, but I can tell you need some time to get ready. Why don't you head into the bathroom, do a little something with your hair and throw on some make up? I keep a little bit in the bathroom, just in case. Me and Troy will start loading the car, okay?" I asked gently with a smile.

"Yes, you're right Rosie, I'm sorry. I haven't dated in so long, I guess I'm just a little on edge. I don't want my heart broken again," she admitted.

"No one does. Unfortunately, that's the risk when we take a chance on love. But when those times pay off, they're completely worth it," I encouraged her.

"Someone should take their own advice," Lily piped up from behind Troy and walked into the room.

"I will throw that entire wedding cake at you," I threatened, but it didn't faze her.

She snorted and rolled her eyes at me.

"I would love to see you try and do that," Troy chuckled and Lily shot him a look.

"Okay, that's enough. I'm going to get ready. Rosie and Troy, go ahead and start loading everything. Lily, I need you to frost some cupcakes I made early this morning. I didn't get to it. I was only able to get out the cinnamon rolls, muffins and scones."

"Sure thing, Mom," Lil nodded. "What flavors did you make? I need to write it on the board."

"Chocolate-chocolate, key lime, vanilla-vanilla, white-chocolate raspberry, and Creamsicle. I made all the frostings and fillings, but didn't get to putting them all together. It's all in the fridge." Mom pointed and stood. "I'll be done in about ten minutes. We're going to be late if I take any more time than that."

"Don't rush, Mom. Just focus on you for a few minutes so you feel better," Lily told her and smiled.

"Thanks." She toward the bathroom, mumbling something about wanting this day to be over already.

I was glad I wasn't the only one feeling that way. Once I saw her shut the bathroom door, I turned to Lily. "Why do you have to be so obnoxious? Seriously, you're driving me crazy today. I cannot wait for this stupid wedding to be over, so I can stop being pestered about this whole Nick thing! Then you won't be able to say anything because he'll be married- and you won't be able to do anything about that!" I marched to the refrigerator to collect the many boxes of treats and load them in the car.

I heard Lily and Troy exchange a few words behind me, but didn't bother listening. I'd heard enough from her and it was only 7:30 in the morning.

I walked the boxes to the front of the bakery where Mom's car was parked. Luckily, she had already unlocked it so I opened the hatch and start stacking the boxes carefully. Troy came up behind me with an armful and placed his stack next to mine.

"Your girlfriend is getting on my nerves," I muttered and walked back to the bakery.

Troy laughed and called out, "She can be fun, can't she?"

"Those are not the words I was thinking of," I growled and stomped inside.

Troy and I continued loading the car until every last pastry box was accounted for. By the time we finished, Mom had emerged from the bathroom, looking like a new woman. "Perfect timing, Mom, we need to carry the cake out to the car. By the way, you look beautiful. Do you feel better?"

"Actually, I do. Troy, can you help me carry the cake out? Rosie, you hold the doors open," she instructed and we jumped into action.

There was always nervousness and pumping adrenaline when carrying out a cake; it only took one misstep and the cake would fall over. An accidental bump could knock off a flower or two or result in fingerprints on the sides of the cake. This was especially true when it came to supporting a six-tiered wedding cake. Thank heaven the cake fit perfectly in the back of the car, but the nervousness and adrenaline never stopped until the cake was successfully delivered to the venue in one piece. This made for a really slow car ride, but if it meant delivering with no issues, I was fine taking twice as long to get there.

Once the cake was carefully placed in the back of the car and set so it wouldn't (or couldn't) fall, Mom and I said our good-byes to Troy and Lily, and were off to the wedding.

As we drove, I looked out the window at the businesses getting ready to open. There was no foot traffic happening downtown, which was to be expected because it was Saturday morning. There were a couple people sitting at the café, drinking their morning coffee, but those were the only people in view.

We followed the familiar route to Nick's house and I was reminded of when I had slugged Jake, and how well Nick had taken care of me. The memory brought a smile to my face.

"What are you smiling about?" Mom asked curiously.

"Oh, nothing." I waved dismissively. "I was just remembering the last time I was at Nick's place. I punched Jake's face in." I chuckled, recalling the look on his face. A combination of: disbelief, confusion, and anger. It was priceless and it surfed around on social media for about a week. Jake had made sure to steer clear from me and Lily at school, which made it a lot funnier.

"I still can't believe you did that, although I'm sure he

deserved it," she said and started laughing. "Lily and Troy came over one day to show me the video and it was hilarious. Who taught you how to punch?"

"I took a kickboxing class." I chuckled. "I didn't think it would actually come in handy. No pun intended."

Mom laughed even harder. "You seem surprisingly calm, considering whose house we're going to right now," she pointed out and raised an eyebrow. "What's going on in that head of yours?"

I shrugged. "Nothing really. I just want this day to be over with. Besides, I doubt I'll see very much of him. He's going to be surrounded by family and friends all day long. The last thing he's going to want to do is talk to the girl who's bringing his wedding cake."

"Whom he actually likes," she added.

I huffed. "Mom, not you too? I already heard enough from Lily this morning." I looked back at the cake to make sure it hadn't fallen over.

Luckily, it was still standing straight and wasn't wobbling too much since Mom was driving ten miles under the speed limit. She had even put the hazards on.

"I'm not going to. I was just honestly curious to see how you were doing," she said lightly, but I didn't completely buy it.

"Well, I'm fine. Really, there's nothing I can do, except do my job, that's all," I assured her.

Her hand grabbed mine and she squeezed it.

"I'm really okay, Mom. If anything, I'll hide in the kitchen."

"If you say so," she sang as she pulled into Nick's driveway. She whistled, "This place is huge."

"Yeah, it is. Do you know where we're supposed to park?" There wasn't a whole lot of parking open and I doubted Alisha wanted us to take her guests' parking spots.

"She said there were a couple spots she was reserving along the side of the house for us." She gazed along the driveway. "Ah, there!"

She drove around the house to the side and saw a sign reading "Karen's Kreations". We parked in front of it and walked up to the door, and knocked on it.

"Are you ready for this?" my mom whispered.

"I have to be," I mumbled.

We were greeted by a maid and immediately a couple of guys walked outside and offered to help carry in all the baked goods.

I opened the back of the car and they jumped in to grab the cake- which almost pushed my mom into a frenzy.

"Whoa, whoa, whoa! We'll carry the cake. You guys just keep the door opens and don't get in the way," my mom instructed them.

The guys nodded and shuffled back to the side door and left it open.

"Ready, Rose?"

"Yep, let's carry this thing," I said.

We grabbed hold of the cake, gently slid it out from the back of the car, and carried it to the house. The two men led us to the dining room and we set it on the table.

The house was as beautiful as I remembered. Everything was open and bright, and had been cleaned spotless, easily passing the white-glove test.

The smell of breakfast food was wafting through the house and it made my tummy growl.

"Where is the ceremony and reception being held?" Mom asked the men.

They were both dressed in white shirts and black slacks, just like my mom and I, but also had black vests. One was easily six feet tall, and the other was a head shorter. They looked like they were in their early twenties and I assumed they were a couple of college students looking to make extra cash.

The shorter one spoke up. "Everything is happening in the back. They have the ceremony set up at the rear of the garden, and a white tent set up where the reception dinner is being held. The brunch is on the back patio."

"Great, thank you. Do you boys mind helping us unload the rest of the car… *carefully*?" Mom asked slowly, as if she weren't sure whether she actually wanted their help.

"Sure." Both nodded and followed us back to the car.

With them helping us unload the car, along with a couple of others who had joined us, we only had to make one trip. I couldn't help looking around to see if I spotted Nick; I hadn't seen him yet, but I knew it was only a matter of time and I was so nervous.

When we were in the dining room, organizing the pastries and sweet rolls, a woman strolled into the kitchen and smiled at us. She was a tall woman with beautiful features, bleached blonde hair, and looked like she had walked out of a tanning salon. She was wearing a black pencil skirt, a grey blazer, and black stilettos, and walked with confidence that could intimate anyone.

"Hi, my name is Natalie, and I'm the wedding planner. You must be Karen from Karen's Kreations." She held out her hand and my mom took it.

"Yes, that's me and this is my daughter, Rosie," she said and Natalie shook my hand as well.

"Nice to meet you both. Thank you so much for doing all this for Alisha. She couldn't stop talking about the cakes you made for her. And these treats look delicious," she complimented us and kept eyeing the goodies.

"Thank you, that's very sweet of you to say. I'm glad you came by, because I wanted to know where you wanted us to be and what you wanted us to do," she told Natalie.

Natalie looked at her phone and then responded."So, the brunch is in about a half hour, so I would like it if you two could set up an arrangement of baked goods, and then help serve it to the guests. Also, make sure the platters are nice and full."

My heart began speeding up and my face flushed. "Wait, I was under the impression that-"

"Do you ladies have any questions?" Natalie interrupted curtly.

"When do you want the cake in the tent?" my mother asked and shot me a warning look that meant for me to stop talking.

"We will keep the cake in here until later. Then, while the ceremony is happening, I'll have you deliver the cake. That way when everyone walks into the tent, the cake is there and ready to be cut. Anything else?" she asked with a smile, but I sensed my questions weren't welcome.

"Nope, I don't think we need anything else. We'll start setting up the table. I'm assuming there's an area set aside for us?" Mom asked.

"Yes, we marked a couple platters. Let me know if you need anything else. I'll be around." She smiled. She clearly didn't want us to ask any other questions, because she walked away pretty quickly.

"Mom, I cannot go out there. Nick is out there," I whispered and started fidgeting with my hands.

"Honey, you knew you were going to see him today. You're just going to have to face it and suck it up," she said bluntly and started picking up boxes of cinnamon rolls.

"I'm going to have an anxiety attack," I mumbled and picked up boxes of muffins.

We walked through the kitchen, where lots of catering staff were busily preparing the brunch, and headed past the patio doors. There were a few guests hanging around, but there was no sign of Nick.

Mom and I found the platters assigned to us and started loading them up. Once we were done unpacking the cinnamon rolls and muffins, we returned for the rest of the goodies and stacked as much as we could on the tables. The two men who had helped us unload the car came out with a couple of girls, all carrying a variety of fruit.

It looked like a beautiful spread. The table was big and long, and was set with navy and blush pink accents and gorgeous blue and white china patterned plates with name cards on each one. I counted the seats: twenty plate settings. It had to have been the biggest table I had ever seen, not to mention the most gorgeous, beautifully decorated one.

Guests began trickling in and took their assigned seats. Where they came from, I had no idea. The house was pretty quiet, but that wasn't saying much. I had only been in the dining room, but the kitchen had been pretty noisy with all the cooking going on. I continued watching people walk onto the patio, look around for name tags… and then I began panicking.

"Mom, I'm going to go get some tongs," I whispered in her ear and walked away quickly, before she could object.

I entered the kitchen and saw busy chefs cooking, and searched for some tongs. All the kitchen staff were distracted and before I could ask where I could find some, I heard someone clear their throat behind me.

"Are you looking for something?" a familiar voice asked, and I felt my heart sink to the floor.

I turned slowly and saw Nick, dressed in a loose blue short-sleeved shirt, khaki shorts, and brown sandals. He looked like he was on his way to the beach. He looked so relaxed and comfortable, it took my breath away. I had forgotten that he had asked me a question and shook my head to clear my thoughts.

"I was looking for some tongs. I need them for the muffins and cinnamon rolls and whatnot." I motioned backward with my thumb and Nick nodded.

He looked as if he'd been caught off guard. My heart began racing and I wondered if there was something on me or in my teeth, but then I remembered this was probably the most dressed up he had ever seen me. This realization only made my heart race faster.

He closed his eyes for second, as if remembering how to speak, and finally responded. "Oh, okay, hang on." He walked across the kitchen casually, reached into a drawer, and pulled out a air of tongs. He handed them to me and smiled. "There you go. Do you need anything else?"

"No, I think that's it. Thank you." I smiled sheepishly and walked away so fast, I was almost jogging. Which was not easy to do considering the type of footwear I'd chosen to wear.

I found Mom waiting by the tables, talking with Natalie again, and handed her the tongs. "Here you go," I breathed and watched Nick walk outside to take his place next to Alisha at the table.

He took her hand and set it gently on the table as they waited for their family and friends to join them.

Once everyone had sat down, different waiters and waitresses came out and filled their glasses with water and took requests for other drinks. Conversations were happening all along the table, so I couldn't make out any one in particular. They had placed our station a good twenty feet away to give the table a little bit of privacy, which was just fine with me. I only wished I was farther away.

Natalie was standing off to the side, looking at her phone and occasionally scanning the brunch to make sure everything was going well. The waiters and waitresses stood behind the chairs of the guests and waited to be called on when they were needed. Once everyone had received their preferred drinks, the waiters disappeared and returned with plates of the most delicious looking eggs benedict I had ever seen.

"I guess you have to make sure you eat well on the day of your wedding," I mumbled to my mother, who was standing calmly, waiting for someone to come to our table.

"Of course. They need enough energy for the wedding night," she stated and I choked on my own spit and started coughing- loudly.

I turned away from the food and bent over to release the spit in my airway and I felt Mom pat my back.

"Is she okay?" a deep voice asked..

I rolled my eyes because I knew who it was and the last thing I wanted was for him to be over here.

"Oh, yes," my dear mother assured him. "Rosie just realized that sometimes the truth is too hard to swallow."

She was mocking me, and I couldn't retort- or breathe- because Nick was standing right there.

"Oh, okay," Nick said warily. "I heard her coughing really badly and wanted to make sure she was alright. I'm glad she is."

I heard him walk back toward the table and straightened up once I felt like I could talk again. I looked at the table and saw that Alisha was eyeing me suspiciously, but then got bored and turned her attention back to the guests.

"You know, that wasn't necessary. Talk about kicking someone while they're down," I deadpanned and cleared my throat. "Man, I really did a number on myself."

"Yes, you did. Get it together, Rosie," Mom ordered in a hushed tone and turned back toward the guests.

Some people had finished their eggs benedict and were approaching the table for fruit and good old carbs provided by yours truly. The women preferred the fruit and congregated by the fruit platters; a lot of the guys requested the yummy stuff. We were busy for a few minutes, filling up plates with the desired baked goods. Nick hung back and let his guests get first pick and once everyone had gotten what they wanted, he came up to the table and smiled at me.

"I see you survived. Were you sneaking a little bite for yourself over here?" he teased and I couldn't help but laugh.

"No." I shook my head. "Apparently, I just can't swallow. What can I get for you?" I hoped to keep our conversation to a minimum. I didn't want Alisha getting suspicious of anything and her going bridezilla on me.

"What do you recommend?" he asked curiously and raised an eyebrow. Clearly, he wasn't getting the hint, or was ignoring it.

"Well, personally, I'm a cinnamon roll fan. You can't go

wrong. If you're not a fan of cinnamon, go for the orange. Plus, I always like an excuse to have frosting for breakfast." I shrugged innocently. "Next, I would choose muffins. The lemon-poppyseed has a yummy lemon glaze on it, but again, I love frosting."

Nick chuckled and scanned the yummy goodies in front of him. "They look delicious, but I'll take your word for it. I would like a cinnamon roll, please."

I dished one up on a plate and handed it to him. "There you go. Hope you like it." I gave him a half smile and waited for him to leave, but he hesitated, as if he wanted to say something. Before he could, I cut him off. "I'm going to get another box of cinnamon rolls. Those seem to be popular. Should I get anything else, Mom?" I asked her quickly.

Her brow creased and she answered slowly. "Maybe some scones? I think people are liking those too." She tilted her head at me ever so slightly, just enough for me to notice, but I ignored it.

"Great, I'll be back." I nodded at Nick before shuffling inside to grab a couple extra boxes of baked goods. I passed the kitchen where chefs were clearing breakfast and preparing for dinner and rushed into the dining room, not relaxing until was on the other side of the wall, alone.

I leaned against the wall, and took a deep breath and pulled myself together. "This is going to be a long day," I muttered. I straightened out my clothes and wiped makeup from underneath my eyes, and then began searching for the right boxes to bring back to the table.

As I was looking for the scones, I saw a figure out of the corner out of my eye and jumped. I focused and realized it was Nick, and I put my hand on my chest. "Holy crap, Nick," I exhaled. "I think I just jumped out of my skin."

"Don't worry, you didn't. You almost hit the ceiling, though, you jumped so high," he chuckled and crossed his arms. "What are you doing in here?"

"Getting some more cinnamon rolls and scones for the table," I reminded him and went back to looking for the scones.

"I think we both know that's not the truth. Not entirely, at least." He took a step forward and inclined his head toward the boxes. "I think you used it as an excuse to get away from me."

"Psshh." I waved him off and then stammered, "I-I… well… the table was running low and w-we needed more. It's my job today, after all. Natalie said she wanted to make sure we were filling the trays so they looked nice and full," I informed him as matter-of-factly as I could manage and picked up the box of scones.

Nick took another step toward me and I froze; he was only five feet away now. "I don't buy that, Rose."

"Well, what do you want me to say, Nick?" I asked, exasperated. He was making me nervous, being in the same room with him *alone*.

"I want you to be honest with me and tell me the truth," he said flatly and took another step forward. Now he was four feet away.

"Nick! You're getting married today. I'm here to cater and provide the cake. Once that cake is delivered to the white tent, I'm out of here, and you'll never see me again. I don't want Alisha to see you talking to me because I don't want her to get suspicious of anything and ruin your chances with her. So, please, go back to your guests and get ready for tonight," I pleaded and tried to sidestep him, but he moved in front of me, now only three feet away.

"Most of the bridal party is gone. Alisha went to get ready. She's not going to reappear until she walks down that aisle. She's pretty strict about me not seeing her before the wedding. The rest of the family is talking about heading into town to do some shopping before the wedding and some of the bridesmaids went off with Alisha. Oh, and a couple of guys are out back playing basketball. Other than that, there's no one here, besides the workers putting everything together, and you and me. None of the guests or family members are going to want to come near a kitchen today. They're all looking forward to being pampered and not having to deal with cooking or cleaning," he explained.

"Don't you think people are going wonder where you're at?"

He shook his head. "I told them I had some things to take care of before the wedding, and that I wanted to spend time by myself." He took another step forward and was only two feet away.

I shuddered slightly, feeling uncomfortable with how close he was. "Nick," I whispered, and he gently took the boxes out of my hands and set them on the table. I looked at him and stared into his eyes, and they looked… calm.

He gave a crooked smile and took my hands in his. "Rosie, run away with me," he said softly.

"What?" I gasped, removing my hands from his and covering my mouth, shaking my head. "Are you crazy?"

He chuckled. "Well, maybe. Rosie, I love you," he confessed quietly. "I've loved you since the first moment I met you. I've tried to fight it, and be respectful considering my situation, but I can't ignore it anymore. I want to be with you."

"Yep, you are crazy," I decided and turned, so I couldn't see him. I couldn't believe the words coming out of his mouth. "I haven't heard from you in weeks and now, on the day of your wedding, you're telling me you love me? Do you realize how insane that sounds?" I turned back to see his facial expression.

He still looked as calm as a cucumber. "I know, I know. I told you, I just tried to push through and do the right thing with Alisha, but I can't go through with it. I can't marry her, knowing that I love you. I would question my marriage for the rest of my life. I need you in my life. I've missed you, ached for you.

"I tried so many times to call you and pick up the phone, but couldn't bring myself to do it. After our last conversation, I was scared, but seeing you again has just affirmed my feelings for you. I love you, Rosie. So much. I know we haven't known each other very long, which makes this even crazier, but when you know, you know." He took one last step toward me and embraced me.

I was rigid at first, unsure of how to react, but feeling his arms around me, his warmth made me melt like butter. For a moment, everything was perfect, and I had the man of my dreams. Then, something snapped, and I remembered that in a few short hours, he was supposed to be standing at the end of the aisle, waiting for Alisha, and marrying her in front of her friends and family.

"No!" I pushed him away. "I won't. We can't do this. I would never do this to anybody. It's not fair to Alisha, or anyone else. You proposed and agreed to marry Alisha. Now you need to go through with it." I could feel tears well up in my eyes, but I blinked them away. I wanted to appear strong as I could, even if I was crumbling on the inside.

"I was blind before, Rosie. I was marrying Alisha for reasons that were not right. It was going to be a loveless marriage, and I think you saw that when she came to the bakery, the very first time we met. You all noticed that we just didn't work. But *I* didn't realize it until I met you and, now, I know what love really feels like," he professed to me, but I couldn't stand to hear anymore.

"Nick, I can't. I'm sorry." I willed myself not to cry, but a tear escaped and I quickly wiped it away.

"Don't you love me?" he asked gently. "I know you do. I can see it in your eyes. Don't you want to be with me?"

I stood there and had an inner debate. A part of me wanted to tell him yes, jump into his arms and run off to Europe with him. It would be so easy to give in and be with him. It was what I'd wanted for weeks, but I was forcing myself to stay away from him. The logical part of me knew that this was right; he had made a commitment to Alisha and he needed to honor it, no matter how nasty she could be. It was the *right* thing to do.

"No. Marry Alisha. You two will be perfect together." I sniffed, tears now flowing down my face.

"Rosie-"

"After today, you'll never see me again. That's my final answer," I stressed and ran from the room before he could say another word.

I ran into someone as I raced from the and almost fell to the ground, but was caught in time. "Rosie? Are you okay?"

My mother's voice rang in my ears, but I couldn't answer. I scrambled out the side door and to the car. Luckily, it was still unlocked, so I climbed into the back and laid down so that no one could see me crying my eyes out.

CINNAMON ROLL RECIPE

3 cups milk
1 cup butter
½ cup sugar
2 ½ tbsps.. yeast
½ cup extra milk
1 tbsp. sugar
1 tsp. vanilla
3 eggs
9-10 cups flour
3 tsps. baking powder
1 tsp. salt
1 1/3 cups brown sugar
1 cup more softened butter
3 tbsps. ground cinnamon
1 tsp. vanilla

1. Preheat oven to 275 degrees.
2. Put milk, butter and sugar into a pot on the stove. Warm the ingredients until the butter is melted and sugar is dissolved into the milk/butter mixture. Do not boil!
3. While the milk, butter and sugar mixture is warming,

activate the yeast. Warm the ½ cup milk in the microwave, add the yeast and sugar. Let it sit until yeast rises,

4. Once the milk, butter and sugar mixture is warm, put the mixture in a mixing bowl and place the bowl onto ice so it can cool down.
5. Once the mixture is cool, add in the risen yeast, as well as eggs and vanilla, and mix with paddle mixer.
6. Put the dough hook on. Add in baking powder, salt and add flour a cup at a time. Once the dough stops pulling away from the sides of the mixture, stop adding flour.
7. Let the dough rise until doubled in size about an hour.
8. Mix together softened butter, vanilla, cinnamon and brown sugar.
9. Once the dough is proofed, transfer it onto a floured surface and roll out until about ¼ inch thick, into a large rectangle. Spread the brown sugar mixture onto the rolled out dough.
10. Start rolling up the dough from the longer side, into a tight spiral and seal the seams. Cut into 1-inch sections with either plain dental floss or a sharp serrated knife. Place the dough rolls onto a buttered pan. Let them rise for another 30 minutes.
11. Bake for 20-25 minutes, until rolls are golden brown.
12. Once the rolls are almost completely cool, put your preferred glaze or frosting on top. Or, use my buttercream frosting below!

VANILLA BUTTERCREAM FROSTING

2 cups softened butter
6 cups sifted powdered sugar
2 tbsps. heavy cream

2 tsps. clear vanilla

1. Cream butter until fluffy.
2. Mix in powdered sugar until combined.
3. Add heavy cream and vanilla, and mix until the frosting lightens to almost white and is fluffy.

CHAPTER 16

It didn't take long for Mom to find me. She climbed into the passenger seat and handed me a few napkins from the glove box. She sat there and let me cry for who knows how long. I bawled my eyes out. I was sure all my makeup was dripping down my face, and my hair was an absolute disaster. The amount of hurt that I felt was indescribable. My heart ached and my stomach was knotted. I couldn't seem to stop crying; I felt like there was no hope left in this world.

After a while, I calmed and took a deep breath. I sat up and looked in the rearview mirror and my suspicions were confirmed; I looked like a sad clown. I used the napkins to wipe my face, but it didn't improve my look. Now, I simply looked like a red, swollen tomato with no makeup on.

I got the courage to look at my mom. She was watching me with a mix of concern, worry and uncertainty. "How much did you hear?" I croaked.

She gave a tight-lipped smile and then sighed. "All of it. I followed you, to let you know they were all done and not to worry about bringing any more scones or cinnamon rolls. Then I saw Nick in the dining room and heard you two talking, and didn't want to interrupt." She looked down, feeling guilty, but I couldn't be mad at her. I'd almost ruined this customer for her more than once.

"Well, I would have appreciated it, to be quite honest. That was not the most pleasant conversation," I mumbled and leaned my head against the headrest. "I don't know if I can go back there," I admitted. "I don't think I can watch him marry Alisha."

"I don't blame you, honey. That was... something." She breathed deeply. "I can call Lily or Troy, and have them pick you up," she offered, but I shook my head.

"I have to stay, Mom. If I leave, it will look weird. Alisha was already looking at me funny during brunch. I need to finish this. Plus, it's not like Nick will be around. He can't afford to disappear again like that, or he's going to get caught. We just need to clean up out there, deliver the cake to the tent, and that's it. Then we can leave and I never have to see Nick again." I tried to sound brave, but in reality, I wanted to run away. I had no desire to stay, but I needed to stick this out. I *could* do hard things.

My mom looked even ore guilty. "Well..."

"What?" I asked sharply.

"Before I came inside, Alisha had come up to me and asked if we could stick around and cut the cake for the guests...and I told her we could," she answered quietly.

"Are you kidding me?" I shrieked.

"No-o" she howled. "I didn't know that Nick was secretly in love with you and that this was going to turn into some big thing! I just thought he had a little crush on you or something."

"Well, it turns out it's more than that," I huffed and crossed my arms. "It's fine, I can do this."

"Are you sure? You don't seem like you're okay and I can do this on my own, I really can," she stated, but I waved her off.

"I'm sure, Mom. Tell you what. If something else happens, or I just can't keep it together, I'll call Lily or Troy and have them come get me, alright?" I reasoned.

Mom gave a deep sigh and her forehead creased. "Alright, if

that's what you want to do. Can you tell me something? Do you love him?"

I felt tears well in my eyes and looked at my hands, and started fidgeting. "It doesn't matter what I feel. I refuse to be the other woman and ruin a marriage. Especially one that hasn't even begun yet."

She reached back and put a hand on my knee. "But *do* you?" The woman was persistent when she wanted to know something.

Unable to speak, I responded by nodding my head. "Yes," I finally croaked. "Very much. I've missed him like crazy." I paused to take a couple deep breaths so I wouldn't start crying out of control again. "And it hurts, you know? Knowing that he's been with her over me and regardless of how he's felt, he's still been choosing her. Don't get me wrong, I get it. He wanted to follow through on his commitment, but it still hurts. And he should, he proposed to her for a reason, but he shouldn't have chosen today to back out and decide he can't be with her. Today of all days, he decides to tell me now that he loves me?" I shook my head, feeling anger boil-inside me. "I have a hard time with that, no matter how I feel about him."

"I get that. I understand. But weren't you the one that told him to stay away?" she reminded me and she was right.

I had told him that, and I knew he was trying to respect my wishes. He was trying to do all the right things with Alisha and me, but I couldn't help feeling picked on.

"Yes, I did," I conceded and continued, "He was trying to do all the right things. I just wish he had come to this realization a few days ago. Or a few weeks ago! Not now," I sniffled and looked at her and smiled softly. "Should we get back in there? We kinda left a mess."

"Are you ready to go back in there?"

"Yes," I confirmed. "I can do this."

"Alright, let's go."

. . .

We walked back into the house and, besides the kitchen crew, the house was quiet. Everyone had disappeared to do their own things, which I was grateful for, and it left us to do what we needed to do. We walked through the house, to the back patio, and there was no one to be seen.

The kitchen crew had almost finished cleaning everything off the tables and had started putting things away, so we hurried and went to work on getting the boxes and filling them with the leftover baked goods. Luckily, there wasn't a whole lot left; it seemed as though everyone enjoyed them.

We took the leftover boxes to the kitchen crew and they stowed them away for us. We also took the opportunity to help the kitchen staff clear the tables and put them away. I felt bad I had left the party abruptly and truly wanted to help. That, and the groom had wanted to leave with me and not the bride was something I felt guilty about. I took the liberty to sweep off the patio, and Mom helped clean off the platters so that the kitchen staff could focus on dinner.

From the sounds and looks of it, they were a little behind and the last thing I needed was to see Alisha mad. I took my time sweeping the patio, making sure I got every last speck of dirt. Once I was done with that, I went back into the kitchen to see if they needed any other help, but at that point, they didn't need extra bodies and kicked out Mom and me.

We decided to check on the cake and make sure it hadn't been bumped, but that didn't take long, so ended up sitting on the table and checking our phones. We still had a couple more hours till the ceremony. I still couldn't believe my mother had agreed to stick around and help cut the cake; it wasn't that hard to cut a cake!

My thoughts were interrupted when I heard my mom huff and slam her phone down on the table. She crossed her arms and continued to huff and puff. I swore, I could almost see steam come out of her ears.

"Hey, Mom," I asked slowly. "What's going on?"

"Nothing," she growled.

I snorted because there was no way I was going to believe that, so I asked again, "Mom, what's wrong? Did your phone's autocorrect mess up your text again?" I teased, trying to lighten the mood a bit.

The only reaction I got was eyes narrowing at me. She said, "Ha-ha. It's just this whole..." She moved her hands as if she were trying to pull the words out of thin air, then gave up and slumped in her chair. "It's Hank. I still. haven't heard anything from him. And I'm trying to not be that nagging girlfriend and text every five minutes to see where he's at, but he's still refusing to respond. I wish I knew what was going on or if I did something, so I could fix it. I have no idea what I did wrong!"

"Like Troy said, Mom," I began, "Guys are terrible about communicating. Most guys don't keep their phones on them all the time, especially older ones. Some forget to charge them. Maybe take it as no news is good news?"

"It's kinda hard to think like that, considering we were attached at the hip and now I'm getting the cold shoulder," she shrieked, which I thought was hilarious whenever she did, but laughing was not the best idea at the moment.

"When's the last time you texted him?" I asked her point-blank.

"Last night," she answered quickly.

"Why don't you call him? You have time; it's not like you're doing anything right now," I suggested, but she didn't seem to like the idea.

"No way. I'll just look needy," she protested, shaking her head.

"Mom, it doesn't hurt to try. You like him, right?"

"Well, obviously!"

"Then, call him. Just try... see what he says. You've got

nothing to lose." I picked up her phone and handed it to her. "Go, let me know what happens. I need something to distract me."

She stared at the phone and hesitated, as if trying to decide if it were really a good idea. But then she sighed loudly and took the phone and walked out of the room.

I leaned back in my chair, pleased with myself that I had convinced her to call Hank, but then realized I was all alone in a big empty house. After a few minutes of sitting around, I couldn't stand it anymore and decided to stroll around the garden while I waited for Mom to finish her conversation. Hopefully, she was having one and *not* talking to voicemail.

The garden was even more beautiful than before. Flowers had been freshly planted all around the grounds and huge bouquets of flowers lined the path to where the ceremony would be held. Workers were running around like busy little bees, setting up chairs, tying bows to the backs of them, adding more flowers to bouquets, and lining the aisle with pink rose petals.

At the end of the aisle was a beautiful arch with elegant pink roses and little white flowers hanging from it, creating a beautiful backdrop. It was the perfect scene for a wedding. I wanted to keep walking around, but Natalie appeared with a couple other women by her side, who were inspecting the work being done. Not knowing whether I should be there, I slowly turned and walked away before I could be spotted. As I was, I heard them talking and stopped when I heard them mention Nick.

"Do you know where Nick is? He disappeared last night. Alisha hardly saw him this morning and, when it was time for the brunch, I saw him long enough for him to clean his plate and then he disappeared again," one woman said to Natalie.

I knew I shouldn't have, but I hid behind a large hedge and listened.

"I noticed the same thing," another woman said. "I asked Alisha what was going on, but she couldn't give me a straight answer."

"Do you think it has to do with that other girl?" the first woman questioned.

"I don't know. Maybe. Is Alisha worried about her?" the second woman asked curiously.

"Wait." This time Natalie spoke. "What *other* girl?"

"Nick was spotted with some girl at the drive-in movie theater. It was dark, so they couldn't see who it was, but Alisha found out," explained the first woman. "Alisha said that ever since then, he's been acting funny, and more distant, but he's still moving on with the wedding, I don't know. I mean, we've made it to today, and he hasn't backed out. Maybe it was just an old friend?"

"Or maybe it wasn't," the second girl speculated aloud.

"Wow, there's *another* woman. I wonder who she could be. Poor Alisha," Natalie said solemnly.

I didn't bother sticking around for the rest of the conversation, I had heard enough. I hurried away from the hedge, hoping they hadn't noticed me and all but racing back to the dining room.

I was having a mild panic attack, and started pacing the dining room. My fears had been confirmed; we had been caught at the drive-in theater. Someone had seen us! Luckily, it had been dark enough; they didn't recognize me or else I would have been in big trouble. I wondered who might have seen us sitting in that dark parking lot, and thought back to that night. My thoughts were interrupted when Mom rushed into the room with a big smile on her face.

"You were right," she exclaimed. "It was nothing. He accidentally dropped his phone in a puddle, so he had to get a new one, which was why he wasn't answering my calls, and then he had some family drop by unexpectedly last night. I worried for nothing!" She looked so happy and bubbly, I couldn't rain on her parade.

I forced a big smile and appeared as excited as I could for her.

"Mom, that's great! I'm so glad it worked out. I told you; you had *nothing* to worry about."

"We're getting together tonight for a late movie after the reception! Now, I *really* can't wait for this day to be over," she giggled.

"Glad I'm not the only one now," I mumbled and leaned my head back in the chair.

We were silent for a moment, while Mom was excitedly texting on her phone and I was wishing time would go by faster.

She finished typing on her phone and sat back in her chair and closed her eyes, smiling. "You know, Rosie, when your dad left, I was heartbroken. He didn't even give me much of an explanation; he just had no problem walking out of our lives and I couldn't believe it. Don't get me wrong, you and your sister are the best things that have ever happened in my life, but I couldn't help but feel a little lonely. I felt like I was missing a partner in crime.

"But ever since Hank came into my life, I've never been happier. He makes me feel comfortable, confident and supported, not to mention loved. I hope with all my heart that it not only works out, but that my daughters are able to find the same kind of love." She looked at me thoughtfully.

"You never talk about Dad," I said quietly. It was true; she never liked bringing him up, and when she did, it meant that she was serious.

"I know. I just wanted to help you understand how much I love Hank," she spoke quietly. "And how much I hope and pray you and Lily find partners that will stick with you forever, through the good, the bad and the ugly.

"Those days will come and I promise you, having someone there for you by your side, really makes a difference. I can't tell you how many times I wished someone was there to support me raising you girls and being with me while I went back to school. Would I have traded our time together? Heck, no. But I do wish someone had been there to help me through the harder times."

"I wish there was someone there for you too, Mom. I know it couldn't have been easy raising us by yourself, but you did an amazing job. I hope Hank can be that partner, I really do. He seemed pretty amazing at dinner," I smiled and teased, "Just make sure if you do decide to get married again, that you don't make your own wedding cake."

My mom chuckled. "Oh, I have someone in mind to make the cake." She winked at me and laughed again. "We'll see though. I don't completely know where Hank's head is at, especially since I haven't talked to him all week. I'm really excited to see him tonight, though, to catch up and see where we're at."

"I bet you are," I said coyly and she gave me a playful push.

"Stop it." She tried to look sound serious, but giggled like a schoolgirl. "I'm still your mother."

"Yes, my mother who's dating a guy," I pointed out. "I can still give you a hard time."

She giggled again."Just don't do it in front of Troy, or he'll think it's okay too, and never stop."

"Roger that… he's been loving giving me a hard time lately. Although not as bad as Lily. Troy loves giving Lily a hard time, but he doesn't do it because he thinks he's funny… well maybe not all the time. He likes to get a good reaction out of someone when he teases them. And Lily's always one to be more on the dramatic side, so naturally she has the best reactions."

She seemed lost in thought, but then spoke up. "Lily is pretty smitten with him. I think more than she was with Jake. And I think Troy really likes her. Or loves her, like he professed last week. I think he would do anything for her. Underneath all the teasing and jokes, he really is a sweetheart and seems to treat her well, which always makes a mama happy."

"Yeah, I think so too. They're kinda perfect in a way. Plus, I love Troy and think of him as a brother, so I wouldn't mind him hanging around more," I stated.

"I agree. He's a good worker too. Oh, did I tell you I decided

I'm going to let Brad go?" She asked and then checked her phone.

"About time... that guy was disgusting," I said, relieved.

"I know, I just wanted to give him a chance. I..." She turned to listen to the loud conversation happening in the other room.

I heard voices and tuned-in as well.

"Where is he? He hasn't been seen since the brunch," Alisha shrieked. "I've called, I've texted, I've had his family try to get a hold of him, and we've gotten nothing!"

"Darling, sweetheart," a woman spoke up in a thick Indian accent, obviously trying to console her. My guess; it was her mother. "He'll be here. Maybe his phone died or he went shopping, because he forgot something for your honeymoon. There are so many things that could explain why he's disappeared, so don't stress, my love."

"Mother! Guests will start arriving soon. He's supposed to be here! Don't you think he's cutting it a little close? Face it, he's leaving me. He's leaving on the day of our wedding!" Alisha began crying very loudly and several women started talking and attempted calm her down.

Not long after Alishas's little over-dramatic meltdown, her mother raised her voice above everyone else's so that she could be heard. "Alright, ladies, please go make last minute touches to your hair, makeup, and whatever, and put on your dresses."

Multiple pairs of feet walked out of the room. I peered around the corner and saw two older women standing on opposites sides of Alisha, whose hair was pinned up in beautiful curls; she was wearing a bright pink robe with "Bride" written on the back. I couldn't see her face, because her back was to me, but I could imagine she didn't look happy.

"Elaine, do you know where your son could be?" the mother of the bride asked Nick's mother, her voice solemn.

"I don't know. I wish I did. I've tried calling as well and his phone goes to voicemail. I'm so sorry he's causing this stress on everyone. This isn't like him at all," she insisted. "But if anything, I'm sure he'll show up. He's an honorable man, who makes good on his promises, not to mention I know he loves you, Alisha."

"Thanks, Elaine," mumbled Alisha. From the sounds of it, she didn't sound very thankful.

"I hope you're right, Elaine. Hell hath no fury like a woman scorned," the older woman warned.

Before Elaine could reply, a door opened and murmuring voices spread throughout the house.

"Nick!" cried Alisha. I heard her run toward the sound of a door having been shut.

"Nick, where have you been?" Elaine demanded sternly. "You had all of us women very concerned. *Some* more than others."

Alisha's mother offered a loud "hmph".

"We've tried calling all day and have gotten nothing! What happened?" demanded Alisha.

"I left to go for a little drive, but then an accident happened on the highway and my phone died. I've been stuck in traffic for a while. I'm sorry I didn't mean to worry anyone," Nick defended himself, sounding genuinely sincere.

Hearing the sound of his voice made me yearn for him in a way I didn't know I could.

"See, there's a reasonable explanation," Elaine declared, "Nick, go upstairs, shower, and get ready!"

Alisha's mother cleared her throat. "Yes, Alisha, go upstairs and see the makeup artist to touch up your face. Like you said, guests will be arriving very soon."

I heard Nick and Alisha go up the stairs, which only left the mothers downstairs.

"See, Maneet, there's nothing to worry about after all," Elaine said soothingly.

"Lucky for him," Maneet responded flippantly.

I peeked over and saw her narrow her eyes at Elaine, and Elaine glared back at her. I thought they were going to start yelling at each other, but then Maneet stuck her nose in the air, stomped off, thus ending the conversation.

"Well, that was interesting," my mother said with a furrowed brow.

"Yes, yes it was," I muttered.

CHAPTER 17

Guests started arriving and I was becoming jittery. I started pacing around the dining room nervously and my mom laughed at me. The bridal party was buzzing around the house, figuring out the order of where they stood in line, while guests were led to their seats.

"You're going to make a hole in the floor with all that pacing," she teased.

"You sound like Grandma," I retorted and kept pacing.

"I don't know if I should be offended or take that as a compliment."

I grinned mischievously. "I'll let you decide."

She snorted. "Aren't you just a ball of fun today?"

"Listen, I just promised to help you and finish out the job. I didn't say I was going to be happy about it," I reminded her and signed. "I wonder if all the guests have showed up."

"You have the green light whenever you need to or want to leave."

"It's just a few hours till we go home. I've made it this far, right?" I tried to convince myself that all was going to be okay, but I wasn't very convinced.

"Yes, but in an hour, he's going to be a married man. It's

going to change here very soon," she added gently, but it didn't help lighten the blow.

"I know, Mom," I snapped, and took a deep breath. "I know," I repeated quietly and sank back into the chair.

"You know, I think you're pretty awesome for what you did. It would have been really easy to run off with him and leave everyone high and dry, and you didn't. Despite you not being a huge fan of this wedding, you were very loyal to the bride and I respect that. It shows your character. You're a pretty special lady, and someone is going to snatch you up someday, and treat you like you deserve. I really believe that," she said encouragingly and put hand on my thigh.

"Thanks, Mom," I mumbled.

Natalie walked into the dining room, and greeted us with a very friendly smile. "Hi. The ceremony is about to start, so why don't you guys go ahead and start carrying that cake? I'll hold the patio doors open, and we'll just sneak past the wedding party," she explained and waited for us to move.

We stood and carefully picked up the giant wedding cake, and slowly walked it out of the dining room. We followed Natalie through the first floor and came across the bridesmaids and groomsmen standing in line, partnered up.

At the front of the line was Nick. When he noticed me, his face flushed and he gave me a half smile. I immediately felt my own face turn bright red and put my head down to hide it.

Natalie was stopped by a bridesmaid. Nick had noticed and jumped in front of us and opened the door for my mom and me. I looked at him and noticed sadness in his eyes. I felt tears well in my own eyes. He must have noticed, because he started to say something, looking guilty, but I shook my head. The last thing I needed was him to tip someone off.

We walked out the door and I felt a tear run down my face. Natalie had yet to walk through the door, so we took a break and put the cake on the patio table. The cake was incredibly heavy with its six tiers of cake, frosting, filling, fondant, and gum paste.

Once she came outside, we picked up the cake and followed her to the big white tent which, luckily, wasn't too far away but with every step, the cake grew heavier in my arms. I was thankful once we finally got to the table where Natalie wanted it placed and set it down. Despite the sweat beading my brow and a little heavy breathing from the exertion, I felt relaxed to know that the cake was finally delivered. Now, all we needed to do was cut and serve it to the happy couple's guests.

Unfortunately, I heard the ceremony begin. Once the music started, I stepped outside the tent and leaned against the entry, and watched the string ensemble play. First, Nick walked with two people I assumed were his parents; then, one by one, the bridal party were paired up and walked down the aisle, smiling, and enjoying their time to shine.

Then, as Alisha started walking down the aisle, everyone rose and it was almost painful to watch. She looked beautiful. She was wearing a stark white-lace mermaid gown that hugged every curve of her body in a most attractive way. Not only that, but her makeup was applied beautifully and no one would guess that she had been bawling her eyes out moments before. Her hair was pinned to perfection, along with a long red bridal veil flowing down her back, which had to be a nod to her heritage. She strutted down that aisle, enjoying the eyes watching her, and owning her moment. She was what every girl envisioned looking like on her wedding day.

She walked up to Nick, then he took her hand and kissed it. They exchanged a few intimate words and then stared at each other. Alisha beamed. It felt like a knife to the gut. It was so painful to watch, but I couldn't look away.

Mom appeared beside me and asked gently, "Rose, are you sure you want to watch this?"

"I can't seem to stop, unfortunately," I whispered and grimaced when the officiator started speaking.

She gave me a one-armed hug and slowly rubbed my arm.

"Dearly beloved," the officiator's voice boomed.

It sounded as if there was a microphone nearby, so everyone could hear him; I really wished they hadn't used one. I didn't want to hear anything, but there I was listening and watching the man I loved marry another woman. Tears filled my eyes, as I realized that I really did love him and that I had wanted him to be with me.

I had thought about him everyday, wondering what he was doing, if I was going to see him in passing, and if he missed me. Unfortunately for me, he had listened to me and stayed away. I hadn't seen him at the café or at the graduation ceremony, except for when he crossed the stage and during their family pictures, and I definitely hadn't seen him at the bakery. Now, after all this time, he was standing close by, eyeing his beautiful bride, about to vow to be her husband forever.

"We gather here today," he continued, "to witness this beautiful couple bond in holy matrimony. Marriage is a promise between two people who will trust in each other, honor each other and love each other through the good days and through the bad, for the rest of their lives. Marriage is not to be taken lightly, but to be honored, respected and appreciated. If there is anyone here who objects to this beautiful couple, speak now or forever hold your peace."

The officiator looked around the audience to see if there was anyone who would dare speak up. A deafening silence was the response and Alisha beamed with pride. Nick was smiling, but it wasn't his usual full smile. For some reason, he was holding back.

"Wonderful," the officiator said with a nod. "We can begin the ceremony. Nicholas Edward Bryant, do you take Alisha Kumar, to be your lawfully wedded wife, to have and to hold, from this day forward, for richer or for poor, in sickness and in health, to love and to cherish, as long as you both shall live?"

Silence followed and Nick stood there too stunned to speak. It was a long enough pause that made everyone murmur and Alisha appeared freaked-out. I, myself, started to sweat and my heart raced out of control. I looked over at Mom and she had a concerned look on her face as she shrugged.

I gazed back at Nick and Alisha, and Alisha's eyebrows were drawn as she gently shook her head.

"Alisha," Nick spoke gently, "Can I speak with you privately for a moment?" Alisha's eyes grew wide.

"Are you kidding me?" she shrieked, her look of confusion replaced by anger.

"Come on, Alisha, not here," he pleaded and reached a hand toward her, but she refused to accept it.

"Anything you say you can say in front of everyone!" She crossed her arms. She really was quite the pill.

"Okay," Nick said slowly, looking regretful. "I don't think we should get married."

"What? Why?" she cried.

Guests were zoned in so intently, some were bending forward, as if trying to listen better. This wasn't required, however, because the microphone was still on.

I gasped and covered my mouth with a hand as I looked at my mother and she looked at me in disbelief.

"Alisha, I think you know as well as I do that we are *not* in love. Most of the time, we prefer to hang out with our own friends rather than with each other, and we never agree on anything. Honestly, I don't think I would make you happy and, deep down, I think you know that."

"You have some pretty crappy timing, Nick! You should have said something sooner!" she exploded and her mother came over to stand alongside her and put her arm around her.

"I know, and I'm so sorry. Really, I am. I just wanted to follow through on the promise I made to you when I proposed to you. But, like the minister said, marriage is a bond between two people who trust, love and honor each other. I don't think either of us can say we do.

"When he said those things, it hit me… that we would already be starting out this marriage questioning and I don't think that's fair to either of us. We both deserve someone who we know at the end of the day will love us and be there for us, no matter what. I'm just not that guy for you and I'm truly sorry," he admitted and looked incredibly guilty.

I couldn't believe what he was saying, nor did anyone else. Mouths were hanging open, some were filming on their phones, and others were shaking heads in disbelief.

Alisha was too stunned to speak; she was literally speechless. For a moment, I felt bad for her. No one wanted to be denied like that, especially in front of a full audience, on their wedding day. But then she screamed and stormed down the aisle and her family hastened behind her.

Nick stood by himself and stared after Alisha, but didn't run after her. His family swarmed around him, guests gazed around and talked loudly, probably wondering what to do. Then, after about a couple minutes of confusion, people rose and gathered their things to leave. Before anyone left, however, Natalie grabbed the microphone.

"Hello everyone, my name is Natalie and I am the wedding planner. We are so sorry for the inconvenience of what has happened. Because of the situation, the rest of the evening has been cancelled, but because the food has been prepared, we will be sending people home with to-go bags. We know you probably have lots of questions for the bridal party, but at this time they don't want to be approached unless they come to you and are willing to share details of this unfortunate situation.

"If you all would make a single file line outside the patio doors, we will hand everyone goodie bags. Please exit the same way you arrived along the side of the house. Thank you so much and, again, sorry for the inconvenience." Natalie headed towards us at a very fast walking pace.

I hesitated, feeling guilty that we had been watching the whole thing go down, but figured it was too late now and stayed where I was and watched her approach us with a very perplexed look on her face.

"Hello ladies, I'm so sorry for what has happened. Believe me no one saw this coming," she emphasized, but I didn't believe her, considering the conversation I had overhead from earlier.

"Don't be sorry. These things happen." My mom smiled at her encouragingly but Natalie was hardly paying attention.

She was staring at her phone, texting furiously, and then puffed noisily after finishing her message. "I'm sorry, I'm trying to make this as smooth as possible, but the bride is refusing to speak with anyone, so I'm trying to communicate with her mother," she divulged and then her phone vibrated again and she started texting away.

I glanced at Mom and she raised her eyebrows and shot me a look. "Natalie, what would you like us to do?" she asked and didn't get an immediate response because Natalie was in the middle of the message.

She finished the text and looked up. "I'm sorry; what was that?"

Mom tried not to look annoyed, but it was hard not to be at this point. "What would you like us to do? You asked us to be here to cut the cake and now there's not going to be a reception."

"Oh right, you two are off the hook. You guys can go home. Alisha wants nothing to do with that cake and she doesn't want anyone to touch it either. Again, so sorry for the inconvenience. I gotta go. I have guests I need to get off this property. Things are looking ugly inside and I don't want them to witness anymore screaming," she deadpanned and walked away, texting furiously.

I watched her for a few seconds and finally piped up, "Mom, you got paid right?"

She snorted. "Oh, definitely. I overcharged for the consultation and for the baked goods, and I doubled the price for delivery. Then I made sure the moment she ordered the cake, she paid me in full," she finished, looking pleased, and I laughed.

"Great, Mom, let's get the heck out of here. I don't want to run into anyone and encounter any more uncomfortable conversations," I told her and checked my pockets to make sure I had my phone.

"Let's go. I can't wait to tell Hank what happened today. He's not going to believe it." She sounded a little excited which made me chuckle. She pulled out her phone and keys and started walking, and I happily followed behind.

Admittedly, I was in a much better mood than I'd been thirty minutes earlier. Not that I wanted to see the couple split up, especially in front of everyone, and so dramatically, but I was pleasantly surprised. I'd been fully prepared to have Nick be married right now and never see him again. Then I would go to Europe and find some nice Italian man to help me forget about Nick.

At this point in time though, despite Nick being single, I was not going to approach him in any way. At least not today. I had already denied him once and was not under any impression that he was going to come after me. I hadn't been nice to him the last time I'd talked to him either. My plan was to leave the house immediately and then book a flight to Europe as soon as I could. I wanted to forget about this entire mess and, hopefully, find the a nice Italian man.

We waded through the crowds of unhappy guests to our car and drove away. No one was going to leave without their free dinner after that fiasco. My mom called Hank on our way home to let him know she was available earlier than expected, and I kept checking my phone to see if there was anyone in particular that would message me, but I got nothing.

She drove us back to the bakery. Lily and Troy were long gone on their date. After checking the interior, she gave me a quick goodbye and practically ran to her car to meet up with Hank. Once again, I was left to drive back to my apartment all alone.

I had been laying in bed, asleep, when my sister barged in and woke me up, demanding I tell her about the wedding. She had heard a little bit from our mother, so she came loaded with questions.

I did my best to answer them as best as I could, so she could get out of my room, but she didn't leave for an hour. Unfortunately, after she did, it took me a while to fall back to sleep.

I tossed and turned all night, replaying the day over and over again. I thought about Nick telling me he loved me and wanting to run away together. I pictured his face, pleading with me, and then his look of hurt and disappointment when I told him no. I pictured the look he gave me when he opened the door for me, before he walked down the aisle, and how I told him no again.

It haunted me all night and it wasn't until early morning that I finally fell into a deep sleep and didn't wake until much later.

CHAPTER 18

Weeks passed and I hadn't heard anything from Nick. The first few days, it was completely maddening, because I ended up texting him to see how he was doing and never received a response. I was tempted so many times to reach out to him again, but refrained from doing so. I could only imagine he was trying to fix the damage he had caused. He was probably under the impression I didn't want anything to do with him after I told him I didn't love him.

The thing was that couldn't be further from the truth. I was missing him like crazy. I kept wondering if he would randomly stop by my apartment or walk into the bakery to see me, but he didn't. At first, it felt as if time was dragging but, slowly, as the days went by, I concluded that I was never going to see him again. Mom and Lily were constantly asking if I was okay and if I had heard from him, but my response was always the same. I felt fine, but the more they asked, the more I wondered if I was giving away more than I thought I was when I was around them. I didn't feel depressed, but did anyone know when they were truly depressed?

Besides, it didn't help that both of their relationships were going smoothly. Hank and Mom were always around each other, spending as much time as they could together when they weren't working, and Lily and Troy were attached at the hip. If I didn't know any better, Troy lived at my apartment, except for the sleeping part; that would always be a no-go until they were married. The frequent stolen glances were sometimes too much, but deep down I knew that I was jealous. This was the first time I truly felt jealous that they were in love and had budding, thriving relationships and I didn't. I didn't like the feeling.

In order for me to be distracted, I decided it was time to seriously schedule my trip to Europe. My mother still wasn't thrilled about the idea, but after the spring and summer I had had, I deserved to spoil myself... not to mention there were, a few baking and pastry classes in Paris I was going to attend. I booked a solid week of them, so this made Mom feel a little better.

I was hoping I could apply what I learned from those classes to the bakery, and experiment with some new items on our bakery menu. So, after my week of classes in Paris, I had a week in Italy where I would explore Venice and Rome, a few days in Greece where I would lie on the beach and swim in crystal-blue water, and then end my trip in Spain where I would then fly back home. Once I figured out the itinerary, I promised Mom a copy and that I would follow it exactly and not make any unexpected changes.

It was only a couple days before my flight left for Paris and I was finishing up last-minute work at the bakery with Mom. I was making sure she would be plenty stocked up on everything she needed before I left for three weeks; she'd then have to rely on Lily to do the grocery shopping. This always resulted in Lily choosing the most expensive ingredients and inevitably missing a few items on the list. It was especially worse when she went with Troy. They did not always help each other stay on task, if at all.

A couple weeks prior they had volunteered to go shopping

and Troy thought it would be fun to try different kinds of Oreos. This included buying multiple packages of four different kinds. To help make use of all these cookies, we had a "Week of Oreos", where we showcased different ones into the cupcakes. We had a Mint Oreo cupcake, Golden Oreo cupcake, Chocolate Oreo cupcake, and even a Lemon Oreo Cupcake. It seemed absolutely ridiculous, but the customers ended up loving them and enjoyed trying the different flavors. Troy liked to take credit but, really, he was just lucky it paid off.

I was adding up the amount of chocolate chips we had when my mother walked up behind me and leaned against the door. "I still don't like the idea of you going off alone. Haven't you seen the movie *Taken*? Or *Taken 2*? Scary things happen all the time to young American girls traveling across Europe." There was concern in her voice.

"Mom, I'm going to be fine. I found a hotel across the street from my classes in France, I joined a highly rated tourist group that I will be touring and staying with, and there will be very few times where I will be alone. Plus, I'm not like some stupid actor who chooses to run off with European boys just because they wink at me. That's not the purpose of this trip," I reminded her for the millionth time.

"Well, what is? Why do you have to go now? Why can't you wait to have someone go with you?" she asked.

I sighed. "Because, Mom, I might not have another time in my life where I can do this. Because I feel like I deserve a break and I don't have anyone to go with." I looked her in the eyes and saw sadness in hers. "I'm not going to stop living my life just because I don't have a man in my life."

"I understand that honey, but-"

"Mom," I interrupted her. "I'm not talking about this anymore. I'm going. It's paid for and I'm really looking forward to it, so please just be happy for me."

"Okay, alright I'm done," she surrendered and slowly walked away.

She had become increasingly more paranoid the closer my trip came and it was driving me nuts. I understood her concern, I understand the "why", but I needed to do this. I've never done anything like this and it was time I did. There was nothing holding me back.

The day before my flight, Troy and Lily were in the apartment, watching me pack my suitcase. They both decided it was okay to walk into my room and sit on my bed. It was almost unsettling.

"Don't you guys have anything better to do?" I finally asked after almost twenty minutes of uninterrupted silence.

They looked at each other and shook their heads.

"No," Lily responded. "You don't want to spend time with us before you leave for almost a month?"

"That's not what I meant and you know it. You're watching me like you're never going to see me again or something. I'll be back in three weeks and then everything will be back to normal. I'll be everyone's fifth wheel again," I shot at her and she looked down with guilt on her face.

"Have you-"

"No, Lily," I stated, not letting her finish the question. "No, I haven't and I don't think I'm going to, so please just give it up. Please."

She looked even more defeated. I felt a little guilty being so snippy, but between Mom's pestering questions about going to Europe alone and Lily asking me about Nick, I had had enough. I needed this trip more than ever.

"Okay, sorry for asking," she mumbled and slid off the bed and left the room.

I was alone with Troy. He was looking at me with a troubled expression.

"What?" I asked, sounding slightly exasperated.

"Nothing," he shrugged. "I just don't like seeing you like this."

"Like *what*? I don't understand why people keep asking me

all these questions! Why can't you people just leave me alone!" I raised my voice and could feel tears well in my eyes out of frustration.

"Because," he responded calmly, not fazed by my reaction, "we all love you and care about you. We know that this is not your normal... you've been off ever since the wedding, whether you've noticed it or not. It's been hard to watch. And now you're leaving tomorrow, all by yourself, and I just worry about where your head is at. That's all." He looked at me with concern and love.

I was having a hard time staying mad. "I get that. But I don't think people understand that I need this vacation to try and truly forget about him. Because, yes, it hurts. I feel like I was trying to do the right thing the entire time by not entertaining a relationship while he was engaged. He even offered to run away with me before he walked down the aisle and I turned him down.

"And now that he's a free man, I've heard nothing from him." I shook my head and leaned over my suitcase and stared at the neatly folded clothes packed together. "It sucks." My voice cracked. "I think I really did love him."

I looked at Troy and he had a pained expression. I sniffed and swallowed my sadness. "But it doesn't matter. If he wanted me, I would have heard from him by now. Too much time has passed and I just need to move on, and this trip is just what I need to do."

"I think you do too. The hard part is that we knew he loved you. The timing was just terrible. It just doesn't make any sense that he wouldn't get a hold of you after all this time. If you think going on this trip is what you need, then I support you. I just hope it helps. That's all." Troy smiled at me for reassurance, but it felt a lot more like pity.

"Thanks, Troy, I hope it does too," I admitted quietly and resumed stuffing my suitcase with way too many outfits.

"I better go do some damage-control with Lily," Troy said, sliding off my bed and walking out of my room.

I wasn't sure if I preferred Lily and Troy to be staring at me in silence, or being completely alone in my room. I sighed and shook my head. I was going to be alone for the next few weeks and I figured I better get used to it.

CHAPTER 19

The next morning, I woke up, having endured the worst night of sleep I had ever had. I'd tossed and turned all night, wondering if I was making a good decision by going on this trip alone. I wondered if I'd remembered to pack everything and kept checking my list to see if I packed everything. Then eventually, my brain would go to Nick. I wondered where he was, what he was doing, or if he missed me at all.

I got a total of two, maybe three hours of sleep, and was so groggy when I woke up, I couldn't believe it was already morning. I rolled over to go back to sleep, but Lily knocked on my door and opened it to see if I was awake.

"Rose? Are you awake?" she whispered.

I groaned and lifted my head to look at her to show that I was.

"Wow, you look well rested. Did you sleep at all?" she asked a little louder.

I rolled onto my back and rubbed my eyes. "No, actually, I didn't."

"I'm sorry that I kept bugging you about Nick. I just wish that the whole thing ended differently. You deserve it, of all people." She smiled sheepishly.

"I know, Lily. Thank you. I'm sorry I was so short with you. It's just been a lot to try and handle the last few weeks," I admitted, feeling a little more awake.

Lily nodded. "I know. I hope you really do enjoy your time in Europe and that it helps you in the way you want it to."

"Yeah, me too. Ugh, speaking of, I better get up. We need to leave in an hour if I'm going to make it to my flight on time." I groaned and rolled over slowly and dramatically climbed out of bed.

"You still want me and Troy to take you, right?" she asked.

"Yes, if you could, that would be great. I'm going to go get ready." I stood and started pulling out the clothes I had picked out the night before to wear for the flight. I knew it was going to be a long one, so I had gone with a comfortable pair of jeans, and a baseball raglan shirt with a pair of sandals. I didn't want to deal with the hassle of taking off and putting on socks and tennis shoes while going through security.

"Okay, I'll text him right now and tell him to get his butt over here." She pulled out her phone and walked out.

Troy arrived fifteen minutes after Lily texted him and looked as if he had just woken up. I couldn't help but laugh at the glazed look in his eyes and his hair sticking up in multiple spots.

"What?" he asked, sounding slightly grouchy.

"Oh, nothing," I smirked and paused. "It just looks like you could join one of those zombie movies right about now." I giggled and heard Lily laugh behind me.

"Honey, you really should do something about your hair before we go to the airport. Do you need some caffeine or something? I think I have some soda that Rose doesn't know about," Lily added gently, not wanting to upset him.

"I'm going to pretend I didn't hear that," I mumbled and walked into the kitchen to grab a bite to eat and a couple snacks for the flight.

"No, I don't need a soda," Troy responded, ignoring what I said. "I'll go to the bathroom and fix my hair though."

He ambled to the bathroom and shut the door behind him. Lily and I looked at each other and quietly laughed so that Troy couldn't hear us.

He may be bubbly and outgoing any other time of the day, but he had never been a morning person. It had been pretty funny when we'd discovered he wasn't a morning person, because he always seemed to be the life of the party. Seeing this other side of Troy was hilarious and we loved giving him a hard time about it.

Once I ate a little something, checked my packing list for the hundredth time, and Troy finally woke up, we set off for the airport. Troy was his usual chatty self and shared how his roommates kept him up most of the night playing a new Xbox game. Apparently, it was addictive and they couldn't bear to turn it off, but it resulted in Troy falling asleep on the couch, watching one of his buddies take a turn in the early morning hours.

The closer we approached the airport, the more nervous I felt. I swore I thought I had multiple butterflies flying around in my stomach, making me feel all jittery and anxious. Lily and Troy elected to park in the temporary parking area so that they could help with my luggage. I tried to tell them that wasn't necessary, but they wanted to make sure everything went smoothly before they left me alone. I guess the sentiment was nice, but I was ready to be alone.

I walked up to the ticket counter to check my bags and print my ticket. When the lady handed me my ticket, it read first class and my heart immediately skipped a beat.

"Um, excuse me? There must be some mistake. This says first class and I know I paid for coach." I felt silly complaining that I would be in first class, but I wanted to make sure I hadn't overpaid for something I hadn't meant to pay for, or that they hadn't mixed me up with someone else. It could have been a complimentary upgrade, though; maybe they needed more seats in coach for all I knew.

"Let me see your I.D. again." She held out her hand and I handed it back to her so she could check my reservation again.

After a minute, the lady slid my I.D. back over to me. "Nope, you're definitely in first class. It looks like someone called yesterday to upgrade your ticket," she informed me.

My mouth dropped and I looked over at Lily and Troy to question them, but they both shook their heads.

"Well, then, okay. Thank you," I mumbled and walked away with my very expensive first-class ticket, staring at it in confusion.

"Who do you think upgraded my ticket?" I asked Lily and Troy outside the security line.

"I think I know," a deep voice said behind me and I froze. I slowly turned and sure enough, it was who I thought it was.

"N-nick?" I asked shakily. "What are you doing here?"

He was standing before us, wearing a dark pair of jeans, a light zip-up sweater, and a backpack was slung over his shoulder. The expression on his face was calm, slightly humored, as if he knew an inside joke we didn't know about. Which clearly we didn't!

"I'm here to catch a flight," he replied and smiled, which caused my heart to race.

"Oh, yeah? Where are you going?" I asked. I couldn't help my curiosity. I made sure to cross my arms and stick my hip out, so that I looked irritated. However, that was really hard to pull off at the moment, because I was really more confused than anything.

He glanced at his ticket as if he didn't know and looked back at me. "Looks like I'm heading to Paris first."

My mouth dropped again, which only made his smile grow bigger.

I held up my ticket. "Did you upgrade me?" I asked, sounding-slightly annoyed.

He chuckled and nodded. "I sure did. I thought you deserved to fly across the Atlantic in the most comfort possible."

"Okay. What's going on? You two?," I pointed to Lily and Troy, who had the biggest grins warming their faces. "Did you know about this?"

Troy held his hands up in surrender and I rolled my eyes. I was in no mood for jokes.

They were both still smiling like idiots and shook their heads.

"No actually, we had no idea," Lily answered.

"Which is probably a good thing too, because we would have given it away for sure." Troy laughed and kept looking from Nick to me.

I started to ask, "Well, then how…"

"Your mom called a couple days ago," Nik explained. "We had a long conversation, and she conveniently had your itinerary… which made it easy to make some adjustments… and made it so I was able to copy everything on it for my own reservations."

"She did what? You did what?" I could feel my hands start to shake and my eyes grew wide. "You're coming… you're coming to Europe with me?"

"Oh, yes!" Troy cheered, pumping his fist in the air.

I looked over to give him the stink eye, but he just grinned at me.

"I haven't heard from you in weeks," I was practically screeching, which caused some heads to turn in our direction.

"I know." His face fell a little bit, but he continued speaking. "That first week after the wedding was rough. You wouldn't believe the drama with Alisha and her family, not to mention my family, although my mom didn't seem as upset as I thought she would be. She seemed more relieved than anything. Once I finally smoothed everything out to the best of my abilities, I finally said my goodbyes to Alisha and I haven't seen her since.

"Then I started work with my dad, which has kept me busy, and I wasn't exactly sure how you were feeling. I didn't think you wanted anything to do with me. You kept telling me to go and that I wasn't ever going to see you again."

My heart fell a little. My worst fears were confirmed. I had pushed him away. He didn't think I loved him.

"But then your mom called and told me about you. She said you had been upset for weeks and she knew that you missed me. She told me about this trip you were going on, and the fact you were going by yourself, so the answer seemed clear. I quickly made some calls and here we are." He smiled at me, but my mouth was so far open, I swear butterflies could have flown in and out.

I whispered, "So, what you're saying is…"

He let out a playful, exasperated sigh.

"What I'm saying is this." He slid off his backpack and put it on the floor, and walked over to me, and placed his hands gently on my shoulders. "What I'm saying is that I love you, Rose. I have since the moment I met you. And I haven't stopped loving you. I've missed you more and more with every day that has passed. But I didn't know how you felt about me and after our conversation on the wedding day, I took that as you were done with me and I didn't want to push, so I kept my distance. But when your mom called, it gave me hope that you may actually have feelings for me.

"Do you? Do you love me?" His voice had dropped to a whisper and I was at a loss for words. Here, this beautiful man was standing in front of me, professing his love and willing to travel across Europe with me, and I couldn't make a sound.

Suddenly, a voice over the airport intercom announced that my flight, well *our* flight was going to be boarding soon. This snapped me out of my trance and I looked at him. His expression was both hopeful and sad, and I realized if I didn't say anything now, I was going to lose him forever, and the thought of that brought tears to my eyes.

I nodded and replied, "Yes. Yes, I *do* love you."

"Well, thank heaven for that; otherwise, I would have spent a lot of money for nothing," he laughed and I quietly chuckled.

"Is that the only thing you were worried about?" I teased, and he shook his head.

"No. I was actually worried about losing something worth much, much more to me," he replied and wrapped his arms around me, slowly pressing his lips gently to mine.

It was as if I were seeing fireworks going off in my brain. My body melted into his and I was lost in a sea of emotions.

We were interrupted by a lady's voice over the intercom, letting us know that the flight was now boarding. He pulled away, but just enough to place his forehead against mine.

"We better get going, or else we're going to miss our flight. I don't want to miss our pastry class," he smirked and I giggled.

"Yeah, that wouldn't be good." I pulled away, but took hold of his hand. There was no way I was letting him go again.

He picked up his backpack and we both quickly said our goodbyes to Troy and Lily, who had been recording on her phone. She must have decided to pull out her phone once she realized what was going on. I imagined they were filming it for our mother.

We quickly ran off to security, rushed through, and rushed to our gate.

"I can't believe you're here," I said once we settled down in our very comfortable first-class seats.

"There's no other place I would rather be," he responded and kissed the back of my hand.

EPILOGUE

THE SWEET LIFE

Europe was a dream! It was everything I hoped it would be, and then some. Obviously, I hadn't anticipated Nick showing up to help escort me throughout Europe. That had been a huge plus.

He was a perfect gentleman too the entire time. We stayed in separate rooms, he opened doors for me, and treated me with more love and respect than I had ever experienced. Then he surprised me in Greece while we were lying on the beach and proposed. So, not only did I not anticipate anyone going on the trip with me, I definitely didn't expect to be engaged three weeks later. I came home to very excited family members.

Troy took the first opportunity to tease him and asked, "So, Nick, are you going to follow through with this one this time?"

Lily promptly hit him in the arm, followed by my mother shooting him a look. I looked at Nick, concerned with his reaction, but he just smiled.

"Oh, yes, I plan on finishing the entire ceremony with this one." He looked at me and kissed my head. "Just as long as she'll have me."

"Always," I smiled back and we gave each other a quick kiss, which made my mother and Lily squeal.

After about a week being back home and finally feeling like I was over my jet lag, my mom had another surprise for me. I had decided to take an additional week off from the bakery, just so I could get settled back into life, including my sleep schedule, which Nick suggested since I was not used to traveling like he was.

I was glad I had, but I was anxious to get back to the bakery to practice making macarons and eclairs from the pastry classes I had had in Paris.

I was preparing all my ingredients when my mother walked into the room and sat in the chair opposite of where I was working.

"Hey, honey, do you have a minute?" she asked, which took my attention away from my baking.

"Yeah, yes, I do. What's up?" I sat in the chair opposite and waited for what she wanted to tell me.

"Well, I think it's time for me to finally step down from Karen's Kreations and let you take the reins," she informed me with a big grin, and I was completely taken by surprise.

"Oh, Mom! Really? Are you sure?" I questioned, but she only laughed.

"Yes honey, it's time for me to slow down, not work so much, get ready for some future grandchildren, and enjoy life with my future husband," she explained.

"Well, if that's what you want to do, I don't blame you. You've worked so hard for so long and…wait, what?" I squealed and peered down at her hand.

On her left ring finger, sure enough, sitting majestically on it was a huge diamond.

I looked at her, my mouth open. Finally, I exclaimed, "Mom! Did Hank propose? Oh my gosh! Congratulations!" I ran around the table and gave her a big hug. "When did he propose?"

"Oh, last night. I kind of knew it was coming, just not when, and it made me realize that I wanted a little more flexibility in my life. Plus, you do such an amazing job here, I hardly do anything anymore. You're going to do amazing things. And don't worry, I'll still come in occasionally and get my baking fix in. I'm looking forward to making your wedding cake in fact. Have you started any kind of wedding planning yet?"

I shrugged. "Not much. I was so tired last week, I didn't do much of anything. I plan on starting it soon. I know we talked about having a December wedding, so four months away? That's doable, right?"

"Oh, sure, sure it is. Just as long as you're okay if Hank and I get married first. We don't want to do anything big, just something small, once all the leaves change color. I think we were thinking October. So, just a quick two-month engagement. Would that bother you?" she asked and I quickly shook my head.

"That wouldn't bother me at all! I think that's a wonderful idea. I can't wait! We're going to have a busy couple of months, you and I," I pointed out and Mom nodded in agreement.

"We sure are. Especially since Troy asked me for permission a couple days ago to marry Lily. I think we're all going to end up getting married back to back," she chuckled and I clapped my hands in excitement.

"No way! Oh my goodness… this is so crazy! And amazing! When is he going to do it? I need to call him. I want to be there when he does it!"

"You do that and let me know too. Isn't it amazing Just a few months ago, even a few weeks ago you were slumming around here, sad as could be and…"

"It feels like my whole life has been turned around, but in the best way possible," I interrupted. "It's pretty amazing. I didn't think I would be engaged for years down the road. I've hardly dated and now I found the love of my life in one of my favorite places in the world, doing what I love. It's amazing how fast things can change and now I have this sense of hope."

"I know, it makes you appreciate what you have, because things can change within a moment. And now, I have no doubt that you're going to live a wonderful, full life with Nick. The thought of you being loved and taken care of for the rest of your life, the way you deserve, just makes me so happy, you have no idea," she stated with tears of joy filling her eyes.

"Yeah, I'm thinking life from now on is going to be pretty sweet." I smiled at my little joke, and Mom rolled her eyes and chuckled.

"Yep, I think so too."

Dear reader,

We hope you enjoyed reading *The Bakery Booking*. Please take a moment to leave a review, even if it's a short one. Your opinion is important to us.

Discover more books by Morgan Utley at https://www.nextchapter.pub/authors/morgan-utley

Want to know when one of our books is free or discounted? Join the newsletter at http://eepurl.com/bqqB3H

Best regards,

Morgan Utley and the Next Chapter Team

ACKNOWLEDGMENTS

When I first started writing, I never imagined the amount of time and work it took to actually finish it. After finishing my first novel, *The Second Chance,* I was so excited, I finished writing this book in three months. However, I couldn't have done it without some wonderful people in my life.

First off, I have to thank my husband John, who in between all his hours of school still finds time to help me with my writing. He helps with the kids, cleans the house and makes some amazing pancakes when I can't get around to making dinner. His level of support does not go unnoticed and I don't know what I would do without him.

To my family, for encouraging me and being my lifelong friends. To my wonderful parents, Jeff and Susie, who have loved, supported and encouraged me. To my in-laws, Wendy and Chad, who love me as one of their own and have become a huge part of my support system.

To my sisters, who dealt with me my entire childhood and love me no matter what, through the good, the bad and the ugly. They were a huge inspiration for this book and without them, I couldn't have written it. They are truly my best and closest friends.

Finally, to all those who took the time to read my book and offer me suggestions, Sherrida Bryant, Kirstin Glenn, Susie Glenn, Wendy Utley and Sarah Villarreal. Thank you for everything you have done.

ABOUT THE AUTHOR

Morgan Utley was born and raised outside the city of Portland, in the lush green state of Oregon. Morgan is currently residing in Orem, Utah, where she is raising four handsome boys, while supporting her husband through medical school. She considers her faith and family to be of the most important parts of her life. If she isn't chasing her boys around, you can find her outside enjoying a run, or in the kitchen baking up something sweet. Morgan is also the author of *The Second Chance.*

Printed in Great Britain
by Amazon

10082696R00130